the
HERO

OTHER DELL YEARLING BOOKS YOU WILL ENJOY

WHITE WATER, *P. J. Petersen*

FROZEN STIFF, *Sherry Shahan*

JUMP SHIP TO FREEDOM
James Lincoln Collier and Christopher Collier

TUCKET'S TRAVELS, *Gary Paulsen*

THE RIVER, *Gary Paulsen*

NIM'S ISLAND, *Wendy Orr*

STORM WARRIORS, *Elisa Carbone*

THE WANIGAN, *Gloria Whelan*

TROUBLE DON'T LAST, *Shelley Pearsall*

SONG OF SAMPO LAKE, *William Durbin*

the HERO

ron woods

A Dell Yearling Book

Published by
Dell Yearling
an imprint of
Random House Children's Books
a division of Random House, Inc.
New York

Visit us on the Web! www.randomhouse.com/kids

Educators and librarians, for a variety of teaching tools, visit us at
www.randomhouse.com/teachers

ISBN: 0-440-22978-2

Reprinted by arrangement with Alfred A. Knopf

Printed in the United States of America

December 2003

10 9 8 7 6 5 4 3 2 1

OPM

This story is for Dad, a master storyteller.

With a special and profound thanks to Tracy Gates, whose twelve years of support and encouragement guided The Hero *into print.*

one

At the time, I had no way of knowing all that my plan would set in motion.

The problem was, I was behind in my weeding. And tired of it, too. So, leaning on my hoe, cursing the heat, looking at the river, and wishing the raft was finished so I could float away from this boring garden, I'd come up with a plan. A dandy.

I'd worked pretty hard most of the summer, wearing last spring's new hoe handle smooth and dark like an old saddle—even darker than my summer-brown skin. But I hadn't kept up very well lately, and now the weeds were winning. I didn't like that.

The instant the idea hit me, I cried, "Ha-e-e-e-ah!" in a fierce but muted shout, my neck cords taut like I'd once seen a movie Judo warrior do as he struck an enemy across the neck and pitched him headlong into the sea. I vaulted into the air and brought my hoe down in a savage chop, sending the nearest button weed to simultaneous death and burial in an explosion of dust. The hoe dropped to the ground like a broken spear as I headed to the granary for the matches.

The squeaky hinges on the yard gate startled Keno awake from his shady afternoon nap, and he gave me one of his barks with a question mark on it.

"Shhhhh," I said. "Be quiet, black buzzard." I didn't want Mom or my little sister, Marie, to know what I was up to just yet. Keno put his head back down, not because of my command but for lack of interest. I routinely dragged the sprinkler to a new spot on the grass as I went around the house.

I got the matches and a shovel. Then, because I couldn't resist, I detoured around behind the granary for a glance at my half-finished raft on the river's edge, a project still of less beauty than promise.

Over two or three summers I'd gathered materials— old boards from Dad's leftover jobs around the place and small logs from the river. After wiring and nailing some of these scraps together, I had a raft that looked pretty good on the ground. But in the water it wasn't to be trusted, and I wasn't about to risk my life on it until it floated better than it did now.

Fortunately, my cousin Jerry would show up tomorrow to spend a week with me. Our main task would be the raft—and that would help a lot.

I was determined that another summer wasn't going to end before that raft got on the river. But we had to hurry. School would start in just eighteen days, and that fact hung over me like a judgment.

The tail end of summer can be a hard time. Not that

school is so bad, really—especially this fall, when I'd be a freshman and take the twenty-mile bus ride each day to the high school in Emmett. But summer's freedom comes to an end, so it's bittersweet—school's starting is—like something dying and something being born at the same time.

The big Payette River—higher this summer than usual and flowing not thirty feet behind the granary and our other outbuildings—beckoned me through shimmering heat waves. I took a second to skip a rock on its glassy surface. I remembered how in June, when the riverside cottonwoods shed their white fluff, this stretch of quiet water below the logjam looked like a field of snow. Rocks skipped across it then made a momentary thin trail before the whiteness closed in again, like the river never knew the rock had been there.

I wanted to climb out onto the logjam—a good source of raft materials and one of my favorite places to be, although at times it scared me to death—but that would have to wait, too. Dad always made clear that work came before play. And right now, I was very excited about work—at least about my new idea for weeding.

I hurried back around the house to the garden, which lay east across the dirt road from our house. As I passed Keno, I said to him in my best imitation of Uncle Remus, "You hain't seen nothin' yet, Br'er Dog. Today, you is g'wan to see things the likes of which hain't ne'er been seen in these parts afore."

He paid as little attention as ever when I played my language games with him. He didn't even open one eye. Over his long life with me, Keno had endured my various attempts at dialects and accents, made-up vocabulary, and speaking in unknown tongues—silly things I did when no one else was around. He'd heard my orations on all manner of sense and nonsense—though he didn't seem to much distinguish between the two.

With no wind, it seemed to be an absolutely perfect day for burning. I struck a match and dropped it into the dry grass between the garden and road.

Poof! A circle of flame spread in every direction so fast it startled me. But with my shovel ready, I walked beside the flames as they ate their way rapidly along the five-foot strip. "This is great," I said to myself. It was exciting to see more weeds killed in two minutes than my hoe could chop in two days. Hearing them hiss and crackle as they shriveled into blackened clumps brought me intense pleasure. Fire was a splendid thing.

I didn't fool myself that I was really doing much good. I could only use fire around the outer edges of the garden, and I never hoed there, anyway. But I told myself that this outside strip was where the weeds went to seed, and getting rid of them would help in the long run.

Frenzied grasshoppers flew out of the way of the flames like helicopters evacuating a bombed city. For sure, no more seeds would come from this patch this summer, and no tall weed skeletons would poke their defiant, brittle heads up through the snowdrifts come winter.

I'd have to be careful, though. Years before, when I was about Marie's age, I'd watched a range fire up on Jericho Flats surge before a hot wind like a stampede of crazed buffalo. Dad and dozens of other men chased that fire, dug around it, and threw dirt at it to no avail. Finally, the wind died down enough for Cats and graders to get in front of it and scrape out a firebreak. It took a day and a half to get that fire stopped, and it had covered hundreds of acres and jumped two roads by then. It was both wonderful and scary to watch.

In the dry season, when western Idaho was made to burn, I was taking no chances. Dad would be proud of me for being careful, but also for my new weeding method. After working all day at the mill, Dad came home to farm our seventeen acres on evenings and weekends, so he had to find better ways to do things if he was to have time to do them at all. And he always got more done than three of me could have in the same amount of time.

I rounded the first corner and headed along the north edge of the garden. This side should be no problem because it was bounded by the small ditch that brought irrigation water from the creek—a ready-made barrier.

But in a minute or two the fire had reached the next corner. *Here's where things could get tricky,* I thought. This east side had no barrier to mark an outer edge. It was a wide open field of cheat grass and weeds, thicker this year than ever because of a wet spring. I'd have to be careful not to let the fire get away from me here, because just a few yards across this field the slope of the big hill began, and dry cheat grass burns like spilled gasoline, especially uphill.

"Maybe I should have dug a firebreak," I thought. But that idea was a few minutes too late. Right now, I was having trouble just keeping up.

I tried to keep the burn about four feet wide, but it was widening rapidly, angling closer to the slope. I started clubbing and digging faster.

The fire was always ahead of me, burning a swath six, eight, then ten feet wide. At one point, the flames crackled a good fifteen feet through a patch of especially thick, tall grass before I smothered them right at the edge of the incline. Wow! That was close!

Anxious thoughts started coming. What if this thing got away from me? There would be no way to stop it before it reached the Big Ranch ditch that cut its way around the side of the hill above me. And if it should jump that, it would go right on over the hilltop into heavy stands of scrub oak. Who could say where it would end up after that? Montana?

My eyes watered and the smoke made me cough. I turned away for a second to catch my breath and was startled to see flames spreading up the slope behind me from the area I'd already worked over!

My mouth went dry. My perfect day for burning

wasn't turning out anything like what I'd had in mind after all.

I was working frantically, but every second I spent here at the front increased the size of the broad black arrow piercing its way up the slope behind me, burning like it was following a fuse. Finally, I could wait no longer, so when the front end finally slowed down, I ran back.

I wasn't one to panic, but my fun had turned to fear and desperation, and I realized help was needed. So while I still beat at the flames with my shovel, I gave up my pride, turned my face to the house, and began to shout for Mom.

The house was fifty yards away, and I didn't know if she'd hear me. I'd last seen her at the kitchen table sewing school clothes, and the kitchen was on the opposite side of the house.

Why couldn't a driver come along—somebody from town or any of our neighbors from farther up the road? I'd even welcome help from Dennis Leeper, if he was capable of any. Why couldn't he pedal by right now on his pitiful old bike, instead of at all those other times when I didn't want to see him?

I even had the momentary, silly hope that my yells might rouse Keno, who, through the smoke, was only a black-and-white smear on the green grass of the yard. If only he'd get up and bark and bring Mom to see what the trouble was.

But not Keno. He might open one eye, but seeing no car to chase or snake to kill, he'd just lie there and let the whole countryside burn down around him. A movie dog would wake up and run and scratch at the door, then drag the mother by the skirts to the scene of the danger. But sure as pigs made pork, Keno would never be in the movies.

At one spot, rocks and sparse grass slowed the fire's pace up the slope, and I made good progress. But I'd abandoned the other end as long as I dared. It might have been best to stay where I was, but I made a decision and ran back to the front just as flames there reached the base of the hill.

Sweat flew from my face as I pounded and dug in vain, all the while shamelessly shouting for help toward the house, like a man overboard beating off sharks while screaming at a passing ship.

Finally, I spotted Marie in the yard. She had come around the side of the house and was staring open-mouthed. "Get Mom!" I yelled. "Get Mom out here!" She disappeared through the front door, blond hair flying.

Almost immediately, Mom was out the door and coming across the yard on the run. Suddenly, she stopped, turned, and ran back into the house. In a moment, she came out again with an old blanket in her arms. At the gate she stabbed a finger at Marie—probably telling her to stay in the yard—and ran across the road, her short legs pounding and her dress flying. At the irrigation ditch she stopped and threw the blanket into the water.

By now, the flames behind me had crawled through the rocky area, sprinted through thick grass, and now were halfway to the big ditch. And in spite of my present efforts, the front end of the blaze had a renewed start up the slope in heavy grass that looked like it was begging to be burned. Fire was everywhere.

I felt like sitting down and letting it go. It was too hard. My eyes stung, my throat was raw, my arm hair was singed, and my legs ached from running up and down the hill. I was soaked in sweat, and my hands—that I'd thought so tough from hoeing all summer—were already red and starting to blister from my grip on the shovel handle. What was the point? It was too late. How could we stop it now?

"Jamie! Come down! Let it go! Help me over here, Jamie!"

I looked. Mom wasn't heading for the burning hill at all. She was over by the pigpen, flailing with her soggy blanket. The pen was to the north, against the creek, and to my amazement the fire had a good start across the fifty-foot rocky swale separating the garden and the pigpen fence. It had jumped our small irrigation ditch—the ready-made barrier—like a lion after a mouse.

I hesitated a second and realized she was right. The slope was lost. The big ditch would have to stop the run up the hill. I hoped it would. But whether it did or not, we had to save the pigpen fence.

It was a wire fence, but right along the ground Dad

had nailed long planks up to two feet high against the posts to keep the hogs from rooting out. Brush grew along the edge, and if fire got into that brush, some of which was dead and dry, those boards would burn for sure.

I charged through the blackened area, every footstep lifting a puff of soot from the black earth.

As I ran, I heard a sawmill whistle, two staccato bursts, calling for a millwright to fix some problem. And even though we needed help, I hoped no one at the mill would look down across the river, see the white smoke, and tell Dad to hurry home. I'd rather we took care of this before he saw it. And I didn't know if what I'd done was illegal, but I hoped nobody saw the smoke and called Jack G., the deputy sheriff. He ran a store on the highway up the river, and he was a tough man I didn't ever want to have to deal with.

"We'll have to let the hill go," Mom said when I reached her. "Have to. We can't stop it there." Her voice was different—lower than usual, and controlled. Mom was known as an enthusiastic person in everyday conversation. But in a crisis, she was calm. I'd seen it once when I cut my foot and we had trouble getting the bleeding stopped; another time when Marie was a baby and had a convulsion that wouldn't quit; and again when Dad developed a reaction to penicillin and his face and throat started swelling up like a movie monster. Mom was using that controlled voice right now. "Help me here, Jamie. Over here."

She was already in action, smothering flames with

each throw of her sodden blanket. But it was like trying to stop a flood with a sponge—it just wasn't fast enough.

A flood! That was it! I was a genius!

"Here, Mom. I've got it! I know what to do," I shouted. Our garden ditch could save us. My shovel made four or five quick slices into the sod bank, and in a moment the stream was rushing across the small field.

The effect was impressive. The fire immediately lost its power as its roots were killed. Small plumes of steam rose from clumps of burning grass as the flames hissed out. Only their tops were left momentarily burning, like tiny volcanoes jutting from a miniature sea, until they toppled over and drowned.

Sloshing through the flood, I scooped and splashed with my shovel where water was needed most. Mom's blanket reached isolated spots, and soon the whole burn was extinguished in the little swale. In one place fire had come within a few feet of the fence, but to our relief, nowhere had the wood or the brush been touched.

"Good work, Jamie." Mom's face was flushed and her breath came in short gasps, but her voice was still as calm as if she was talking about what we'd have for supper.

It was a victory whose celebration would have to wait. The main blaze still burned on the hill, pouring out enough smoke to dim the sun and turn the world a gauzy yellow. The whole area above the garden was black now where the two pyramids of flame had joined and were licking their way up the hill. But as I'd hoped, the big ditch was working as a barrier; I saw no flames above it. Having reached its upper limit, the fire now burned sideways around the hill, in two different directions at once.

"Where now?" I cried. I stood there and thought about it and decided the fire would burn itself out on this end because it didn't have far to go before it would meet the green willows of the creek. The one and only thing it could hurt here was Arlie Leeper's pitiful fence. And I wouldn't have given a bucket of potato peels for that thing.

"The flume!" I cried, answering my own question. "We have to save the flume." The south end was where the danger was. A quarter of a mile down the road, the big ditch crossed a steep slide area on the hill. Here, a huge section of the hill had slid away at some time in the past, from several yards up above the ditch clear down to the road. A sheer rocky grade was left where no vegetation grew. Someone long ago had built a wooden trestlework to carry the water across this unstable place. *The flume* is what we called the whole thing.

At the near edge of the rocky slope was a gully with a stand of dry brush. I feared that if the fire got that far, the burning brush might ignite the old timbers of the trestle and burn it down, collapsing the pipe and loosing the mighty stream of water to cascade down the slide and across the road. If that happened, there wouldn't *be* a road anymore. It was a frightening thought and would put me in more trouble than I could manage.

Mom yanked her blanket from the water and we ran

across the garden where we caught up with the fire. We started to work. Beginning at the bottom, we were careful to put it out thoroughly as we made our slow way up the hill. We had no time to waste, but if we kept at it, it looked like we'd likely quench the flames before they reached the brush and flume. We'd have to.

Soon Mom said, "I wish I had some water. This blanket is as dry as a south wind." In only a few minutes, her blanket had turned into a smoking, tattered rag.

It must have taken us twenty minutes to reach the ditch, but it felt like twenty hours. My arms and shoulders ached like I'd carried a cow across two counties. When we finally put out the last of the flames, we were only a few yards from the brush and trees in the gully.

On the bank of the big ditch, where the water kept the grass green all summer, we collapsed to catch our breath. I lay on my back with my arms splayed and my eyes closed. Heaven!

After a moment, I pulled up on one elbow. "There's Marie. Look at her." I pointed to the little figure in blue shorts waving at us from the yard. We waved back until Marie finally stopped. Keno hadn't moved and was still stretched out beside her like an old rug.

I turned to the brimming ditch and splashed water on my face and arms. It felt wonderful, like a summer rain, especially on my arms, where the skin now seemed a couple of sizes too small. I lay facedown and put my cheek on the cool, moist bank, the best bed I ever felt.

After a few moments, I raised my head and looked

at Mom, sitting quietly. Her cheeks glistened with sweat, her hair was a mess, and her round glasses had slid down her smudged nose. She was still breathing hard, staring out across the valley. I realized she'd probably never been up here before. She didn't hike around like I did.

It was a nice view, all right. You could see the river—its surface as still as death from this far up—all the way down to the first irrigation dam, where a froth of turbulent white water streamed out below it. Looking at the river reminded me how much I wanted to finish the raft.

Straight across from us, the railroad tracks were two gleaming ribbons in the sun. And farther downriver, where the valley broadened out, you could see a few of the houses on the near edge of Union, our little town.

In the other direction, over the top of our row of tall black walnut trees, across the river and a half mile upstream, nearly all of the big sawmill where Dad worked was visible, not just the roof and smokestack we could see from our yard.

I raised up on one elbow again and decided to try to explain myself to Mom before she could ask. I told her of my plan to burn the weeds and how careful I'd been, but how the fire had, at last, got away from me. She listened without comment until I finished. Then she asked, "James West, you lit this on purpose?!"

"Yes, ma'am."

She paused quite a time before asking, "You really thought putting a match to those dry weeds would help the garden?"

I didn't answer, and she didn't say any more, but I knew she thought it was a turkey-dumb idea. And I couldn't argue with that. She added, "You have to check on the far end, Jamie. There's Leeper's fence . . ."

"Oh, who cares if that thing burns down?" I said. She waited me out. "Okay, I'll take a look." I sighed wearily and stood up to go.

"Then, if the fire's out, hurry home so we can get cleaned up before your dad gets back. You could use some cleaning," she said, looking me over. "And I suppose I could use a little myself."

I nodded. As I started upstream on the ditch bank, Mom headed down the hill. She was a sight. The housedress she'd never wear again was blackened all over and scorched around the hem, and the blanket dragging behind her looked like a kite's tail struck by lightning.

"Thanks, Mom," I called. She didn't turn back, but gave a weak wave of her arm, like she was shooing a fly. "There'll be some talking to do," she replied.

Just then, the five o'clock whistle sounded at the sawmill. Dad would be starting home. He'd drive three miles down through town and another three miles back up our dirt road. Today, I'd just as soon he'd take his time.

two

I was still up on the ditch bank when Dad got home.

It hadn't taken me long to walk upstream and see that the fire was out. I didn't go down off the ditch bank to check Arlie's fence up close; I wasn't that concerned.

I was ready to head to the house when I heard Keno give two or three short barks from the yard, the way he usually did when he heard Dad's pickup come around the bend down by the Big Ranch.

I could see the dust rising above the riverside trees even before Dad's tan Chevy truck came into view. I watched it come along beside the garden, where it slowed and then stopped in the road.

Dad got out. He walked along the garden with his hands on his hips and stopped where the road had turned into a muddy flood, with water pouring across it and into the creek.

The ditch! I'd forgotten all about it!

I headed down the hill on a run. "Don't worry, Dad. I'll fix it!" I yelled.

He looked up and saw me. "What happened here, Jamie?" he called. "Is the fire out up there?"

"It is," I answered. He watched me from the road for a good minute as I dug out the sod dam in the ditch and worked carefully to build up a good strong bank again. Then he got back in the truck and headed up the creek road. I knew he wanted to see the fire damage for himself. In another minute he was back, and he parked the truck under the locust tree in front of our yard fence. By then I was done, so I met him at the road where he stood looking over the damage.

"So what happened, Jamie?" he asked again.

I took a few minutes and told him the whole story.

He scratched his head and rubbed the back of his neck. His brown eyes looked at me for quite a while, then out across the damage again. "Let me get this straight. You thought burning the weeds around the edge of the garden would help anything?" He sounded incredulous. At fourteen, I was already a little taller than he was, but I didn't feel grown up right now.

I lowered my eyes. "I guess not," I said.

"You were lucky you didn't lose it over the hilltop. We'll have to talk about this," he said soberly, before turning to walk to the house. Dad was always quiet, but never more so than when he was upset.

I hurried around back to put away the tools. I scraped my muddy shoes on the shovel and wiped them on the grass until the bottoms were as clean as new plates. No mud would get tracked in today. I even hosed the mud off the shovel and rubbed it clean with my hands before putting it back in the granary. I hurried because evening chores were my job, and I was late already.

Forgoing my frequent game of teasing the chickens—tossing out five or six kernels of wheat at a time to see them scramble and whip their heads around in frustrated little jerks looking for more—today I cast the grain on the ground in long, wide sweeps like Dad did.

I hurried on to our small barn across the creek, rapping on the bottom of the milk pail with my knuckles as I walked. The cow was ready and came in from the field to meet me at the stall.

Milking fast hurt my hands and arms clear to the shoulder, especially today with the blisters I'd put on my palms, but I hurried anyway.

"Come on, cow, let it down." She probably thought "cow" was her own special name. But at our place, the only animal with a name was Keno. My folks sometimes talked about their early married days, when they ran a dairy herd. Morning and night in those years they'd milked up to seventeen cows—Blondie, Boss, Runt, Kicker, Lucy—named to keep them straight. Now we had but one, and she was just "cow."

On my way back to the house with the milk, I met Marie coming in from gathering the eggs, her only outdoor chore. "Will you be in a lot of trouble, Jamie?" she asked, concern in her voice.

"I don't know. I guess so." My main fear was that I wouldn't be allowed to have Jerry over tomorrow. Then the raft wouldn't get finished.

In the house, I saw that Mom had cleaned up and changed clothes and had cleared her sewing from the kitchen table. I gave her the milk to strain and put in the refrigerator.

Through the doorway to the living room I could see Dad sitting on the couch holding Marie on his lap. Her blue eyes were scrunched closed with giggling as he tickled her with the lightest touch of just one finger. She even went into hysterics when he didn't touch her at all but just pointed his finger at her. I couldn't remember what it was like to be six years old.

"Jamie, hurry and clean up," Mom said. My hair smelled of smoke but supper was ready, so I did a quick cleanup at the sink.

I said little at supper, waiting, because Dad hadn't asked any questions yet. It felt good to sit down. Soon Mom started telling the details of our adventure. She asked me if I wanted to tell it. I wasn't sure I wanted *anybody* to tell it, but I told her to go ahead. I put down my fork and listened.

When Mom told a story, you'd hardly know it was the same thing you'd just lived through. She knew what to leave out and what to add so it was exciting—like some big pageant or movie. Hearing her tell of the fire, I was reminded of the searing heat, the weeds crackling into flame, the sweat dripping off my chin, and the sweet, choking white smoke—almost as clearly as I'd felt, heard, and smelled them just a few hours before, during the real thing. Marie was spellbound and sat with her eyes wide.

I was squirming inside, but I made myself sit quietly, listening to Mom. I spent equal time watching Dad, trying to read his reaction. Mom told of how hard I worked, and how I made the right decision about saving the flume.

Mom could almost hypnotize you with her hands. They were always moving. Her fork became my shovel as she talked about how I dug through the ditch to flood the field and save the pigpen. It made me sound like a hero, which I didn't deserve.

When Mom told a story, she *made* you see and believe. If it had all been a lie, you'd still believe—you couldn't help it.

When Mom finally finished her performance, Dad said, "Quite a story, Evy." He then asked me a couple of questions, and when he was satisfied, he leaned back and said, "Well, sounds like a bad day at Black Rock around here."

I was startled. This line was from a movie title, and it was something he said when he wasn't serious.

"Not much happened at the sawmill today, either. Oh, sure, the big flywheel flew off the main engine, tore through the wall and rolled almost to the highway; the boiler exploded, landing seven men in the river; and the green-chain wing burned to the ground. A few things like

that. Kept us busy as cats a-coverin' there for a few minutes. Otherwise, it was about as quiet as here at home."
Marie stared at him open-mouthed for a moment before
figuring out he was teasing Mom, who clucked her
tongue at him in mock disgust.

"It sounds like you did a good job, you two," Dad
went on, now serious, "saving the pigpen and the flume."
He turned to Marie and winked. "And you, too, honey-
bunch." She smiled and scrunched her face up trying to
wink back.

I waited, toying with my fork, but when nothing
more was said, I glanced over quickly at Dad and went
back to eating.

I couldn't believe I wasn't in trouble. Two or three
years before, when I left the gate unlatched and the beef
calf got out of the pasture, I was sent to bed without supper after we spent an hour chasing him up and down the
road in the rain. In the winter, if I let the wood box on the
porch go empty, Dad would wake me up early and send
me out to the woodshed in the cold morning half-light
before anybody else got up. And when Marie cried under
my teasing, I was sent to my room. But when my foolishness nearly burned up the whole hillside, pigpen fence,
and big ditch flume, Dad didn't seem upset. Maybe he
could tell I'd learned my lesson. Or more likely, it was
Mom's telling it the way she did. Mom used words the
way a carpenter used tools.

Suddenly, I said, "It was dumb, and I'm sorry." It
was hard to say and I could feel my face get hot.

Everyone looked surprised, like I'd announced I was getting married tomorrow, because "sorry" wasn't my usual kind of talk.

Dad turned to me and said, "I once had a fire come close to getting away myself. Scared me." He looked thoughtful but he didn't tell the story, and it wasn't the time to ask him about it right then. "It's good you can admit your mistake," he said. "You're an honest boy—always have been."

Dad seemed about finished. Marie looked at me out of the corner of her eye and smiled—glad, I think, that I wasn't in trouble.

"Well, no damage done," Dad said, "except maybe in one place."

It took me a second, but then I knew what he meant. "Oh, that old fence . . . ," I started.

"We'll have to see, won't we?" He pushed himself back from the table. He looked at me with serious eyes. I turned away and frowned. "He's our neighbor, Jamie." There was no point in arguing. Dad always taught me that neighbors help neighbors. But the thought of having to deal with Arlie Leeper or his fence—I'd rather shampoo a porcupine.

The ride up the creek in the pickup took only a few seconds, and soon we found ourselves standing on the edge of the road looking down at Arlie Leeper's fence.

"Stay here, ragbag," I said to Keno, who had

jumped in the back when we left. I always called him by any name but his own. Maybe that's why he always ignored my orders. He jumped to the ground.

We looked across the creek at the burned area. Five posts had been in the path of the fire, but three of them were in the green growth near the creek where the flames would have found little fuel. They showed no damage but some smoke smudges. The other two were higher on the hill, where tall grass and dry brush had surrounded them. These two were scorched and wisps of smoke still rose from the base of one of them.

"Those two are in pretty bad shape," Dad said, pointing.

"Too bad for them," I muttered sarcastically.

This fence was an example of the problem with the Leepers.

They had moved up to the old Branagan place east of us about a year and a half earlier. Where they'd come from, I didn't know and didn't care. They weren't from around here, I knew that. One of the first things Arlie Leeper did to show his neighborliness was put up this fence where there was no need for one at all. What was he fencing out? Wild boars?

We'd always thought we knew where our eastern property line was. But Arlie checked with the county recorder's office and found that his precious land reached down the creek another few feet below where we'd thought. So he built the fence to make clear his claim to a patch of worthless brush—and probably to wall out the world. That was Arlie Leeper—a man whose specialty in life was un-neighborliness.

"I'll take a closer look," Dad said as he slipped down the steep road bank. He crossed the creek, stepping on the stones exposed by the low summer stream flow, then climbed up the hill a few yards to the burned posts.

While Dad checked the posts, I threw rocks. Flat ones skipped up the hard road and sent up puffs of dust like machine-gun bullets in the movies.

"Look at this one, you speckled hen," I said to Keno as I dusted off a flat stone almost as thin as a silver dollar and twice as big across. "Nine ricochets in this one."

I threw it hard and got six good bounces plus two puny ones.

Watching Dad step over our water pipe on the other side of the creek brought back memories of the trouble we'd had with the Leepers over our drinking water.

Years before, when we first moved here, Dad got permission from the Branagans—our upstream neighbors long before anybody'd ever heard of the Leepers— to pipe our water from the spring on their property, just up the creek from where I now stood.

Then, almost two years ago, the Branagans, a nice old couple whose whole married life had been spent on their ranch, retired at the end of the summer and moved to town. Their place stayed vacant through the fall and into the winter. One day in early January of last year, we saw a broken-down old truck chug by carrying dilapidated furniture. And two days later, before we'd even had a chance to go up the road to greet our new neighbors, Arlie Leeper came to call.

It was a gray weekend morning and Dad had his head under the hood of our Dodge sedan out front, gapping the spark plugs, when Arlie stopped by. I was there and heard it all. And that's when I came to detest Arlie Leeper, the very first time I ever saw him.

The day was bitter and windy, and with my gloved hands deep in my coat pockets, I marveled at how Dad could work with bare fingers.

I was about to go back to the house and thaw out when the ancient truck came down the Branagan road and growled into our parking area. A short, potbellied man stepped out and tracked across the skiff of new snow that had come in the night. He wore dirty work clothes, a sweat-stained old felt hat, and three days' growth of whiskers. The nervous eyes and the threatening scowl were, I later came to recognize, Arlie Leeper's normal, everyday look. He looked like a man who'd had two helpings of chittam bark for breakfast, without sugar.

I watched warily as he approached my dad, then stopped several feet away when Keno barked from the porch, where he'd huddled out of the wind.

"Name's Leeper," he said gruffly and much too loudly.

"Hello, Mr. Leeper," Dad started, wiping his hands on a grease rag. "Welcome . . ."

"I come 'bout the water," Leeper cut in, never stepping close enough to offer to shake hands.

"The water?"

"That you take from my spring upcreek." He made us sound like a regular band of pirates and cutthroats and thieves in the night. "I'll need payment."

Between statements Arlie clamped his lips shut tightly, like he was biting something, which forced hot vapor to steam from his nose in short puffs in the freezing air.

Dad's back straightened a little and he gave Arlie a long look, but then he deliberately laid down the rag and leaned back on the fender of the car. He cleared his throat and waited.

"Figure fifteen dollars a year'd be fair," Arlie said.

A funny twitch danced below one of the man's eye sockets, and his pupils never stopped roaming around in quick little jerks under his heavy eyebrows. They were the strangest eyes I'd ever seen, like those of a cornered animal. They made me think of the weasels that sometimes came out of the river brush and into our chicken house at night, and how their eyes looked when a light was shined on them. You could never trust eyes like that.

From that moment on, it was all over between me and Arlie Leeper, even before it started. I was so mad I wasn't cold anymore. I didn't say a word, but I went over and stood by Dad, facing this mean stranger until he left.

I wanted Dad to pick up a wrench and chase this intruder off our property. But that wasn't Dad's way. He just shrugged it off. He didn't care for Arlie's ways—saying later that Arlie looked like a man who, if you offered him a biscuit and a bowl of beans every time he smiled, would soon starve to death—but the spring was on Arlie's land, so that was that. You worked with your neighbors, that was Dad's attitude. From that time on, we paid for our water—water that, without our pipeline, would have run to waste in the creek, as it had ever since Adam first met Eve.

Later that year the fence went up—to make the point, we guessed, about who owned what.

That January's cordial visit was the only one we'd ever had, fortunately, from Arlie Leeper—except when he stopped by every four months right on the due date to collect the water payment. He wouldn't have been a day late for that if he'd had to get off his deathbed and crawl to our house.

"We'll need new posts, Jamie, for these two," Dad called from across the creek. "They're partly burned through."

I groaned like a man condemned. But I knew it would do no good to argue against Arlie's need for his cherished fence. Dad would say it was his right and we needed to go along.

It came to me in an instant what we'd be doing tomorrow—and it wouldn't be building a raft.

Lots of people in our valley didn't feel quite as neighborly toward the Leepers as Dad did. Most seemed to think they weren't much good. Folks still referred to their ranch as the Branagan place, as if the newcomers hadn't arrived at all—a form of wishful thinking, I supposed.

Suddenly, Keno's ears popped up and he sat up taller on his haunches, looking up the road.

"What is it, old prune?" I asked him. He wagged his tail once in reply and kept his eyes up the road. In a few seconds, I heard it, too.

"Oh, glory and hallelujah," I said to myself. "Just what we need." I turned and called to Dad, "There's Leepers comin'!"

Coming into view around the bend up by the spring was the old flatbed truck, the only vehicle the Leepers owned. Through the dust on the cracked windshield appeared Arlie's perpetual frown.

Arlie saw me and screeched to a stop still fifty feet up the road. With nothing to hold on to, the two or three kids on the back lurched forward until I thought they would roll off onto the ground. Arlie wouldn't have cared.

There were four or five Leeper kids in all, I didn't know for sure. They didn't do well in school or sports or anything—not even games at recess. They mostly just stood around and looked dumb; they were exceptional at that.

They had no mother that I'd ever heard about, and they weren't clean or taken care of. They never bought school lunch, and their clothes looked like they'd been handed down two or three times too many. I didn't even know the names of all the younger ones. Kids at school usually just called them, "Hey, Leep," if they spoke to them at all.

I was glad to see that Dennis, the Leeper that was my age, wasn't along. He was a pest. Dad was always encouraging me to do things with him because he seemed so lonely, but it was near impossible to like him.

"Stay put. You stay put now," Arlie snarled at the kids as his door squeaked open and he stepped down heavily. He left it standing open and marched across the road toward me, glowering. He looked like he'd had his daily quota of crab apples, cores and all.

Arlie was a short, stout man. His belly jiggled with each step, and the dropping sun made his long shadow on the road look like a picture I'd seen of a big jungle snake that swallowed a baby goat whole.

Even Keno didn't like Arlie Leeper, and he barked once shrilly, his nose pointed high in the air, almost like he was going to howl. *Go get him, Keno* is what I thought, but "Be quiet, Keno" is what I said.

"Had a fire here. This here fire burnt up my fence, I see," Arlie growled from twenty feet away, barely glancing toward the fence. "Ruint it." He paused a bit. "Know anythin' about it?" He jabbed his finger at me. I decided not to answer his rude accusation.

He spat in the road. From under the felt hat he wore summer and winter, sweat ran down his cheeks and into the stubble of his beard. "Somebody took and burnt up my fence," he mumbled.

Yeah, we took and did it, all right. Ruint it. Burnt it. You name it.

I was deciding to speak when I heard Dad's calm voice from behind me as he came up the bank. "Hello, Arlie."

Arlie ignored the greeting. "Pret' near burnt my fence to the ground, looks like. Somebody did," he said, peering past us now, looking for damage. "My kids seen the smoke and tol' me. I come to see." Some of the growl was gone from his scratchy voice now that he was talking to Dad. He wasn't quite as dumb as he looked.

Arlie had stopped his forward approach like he didn't want to get too close to the likes of us. He tramped back and forth now in small, quick steps, like a caged animal pacing.

"It's not too bad, Arlie," Dad said, now standing beside me. "Only two posts hurt. Three others blackened a little. Have a look."

"The fire gets in 'em, they're weak from then on, I say. Oh, they're ruint all right, that's gor-un-teed."

"Well, maybe so," Dad said. "Anyway, tomorrow is Saturday, and my boy and I'll be up here as soon as we can get into town and pick up some new ones."

"Need good ones—aged, treated—like I used," Arlie ordered. "I took and used good, stout posts when I built it. This here was a good fence afore somebody burnt it down." He glanced my way.

What a purebred lunatic! Nobody had burned down anything. His precious fence was still standing perfectly upright, and only two posts were hurt in any way. But to hear this man talk, you'd think I was Public Enemy Number One and had burned down the school, the sawmill, and the Ladies' Club Hall, all in one afternoon. Right then, I was sure you could've hid Arlie's brain in a gnat's hind end with room to spare.

The evening light had now turned dim and yellow like old varnish as half the sun had slipped behind the hill way over across the river.

"I did it," I said weakly.

Arlie looked surprised, which I enjoyed seeing. Telling the truth sometimes surprised people. Arlie set his jaw and made a low, growling sound in his throat, like a creature you wouldn't want to meet on a dark night. Then he muttered, "Well, you're honest, anyway." He paused a minute. He'd lost his steam and didn't know what to say now. Then he said to Dad, "Now, use stout posts, like I done. Like them up there at the spring."

"You have any extras, Arlie?" Dad asked. We all knew about the pile of posts that had lain unused up by the spring for over a year now. "It would save us a trip to town."

You'd have thought somebody'd slapped Arlie in the face with a thistle. Suddenly, his hands flew up in tight fists. "Why, man, what are you sayin'? Them's my posts! People burn down my fence, then take and ask me for the posts to fix it with?!"

"Arlie, now hold on," Dad said, shaking his head in disbelief. "You're the one brought it up. I thought you were offering. But don't worry about it; we'll get some posts, all right, and we'll get good ones."

But now Arlie was really worked up. He went on stomping and raging for another minute or two about how people always tried to cheat and take advantage of him. His uneasy eyes, like a pair of blue jays fighting in the air, never lighted.

As Arlie stormed about, he did an astonishing thing. He absently took off his hat, hit it against his leg a time or two and wrung it in his hands like a dishrag. Until then, that old hat always had seemed a permanent attachment. In a year and a half, this was the first time I'd ever seen Arlie Leeper's head uncovered. He had a full head of coarse, oily, dark hair. Where his hat was used to sitting, there was a matted ring, like a dark halo.

Suddenly, he was all done, and he looked down at the hat in his hands as if stupefied at how it got there. He slammed it back on his head. He turned and was halfway back to his truck when Dad called him by name.

"Arlie, one thing." Dad spoke softly all the time, maybe even more so when he had important things to say. I'd noticed that people listened, and Arlie was no exception. He stopped and turned around. Dad went on. "My boy and I, we'll fix the fence, all right. It's the right thing. But let me tell you—it takes the pleasure out of doing the right thing when you take an accident and make it sound like a crime."

Arlie looked stunned, like he'd been smacked in the head with a crowbar. For the first time, those wild black eyes stopped their shifty flitting around and stood still for a moment, looking at Dad. Thinking didn't appear easy for Arlie, but he seemed to be working at it now.

"Well . . ." He hesitated and ran the back of his hand across his stubbly chin, then spat in the road again and jerked himself around to go. Seeing one of his kids had got down off the truck bed, he took it out on him. "Get back on that truck, boy, right now, like I tol' you," he yelled. "Right now!"

The kid scrambled up while Arlie hoisted himself in behind the wheel and slammed the door. The engine coughed, the transmission whined, and the truck backed up the road to a turning-around place, the tires sending up dust.

As the truck backed around the curve and out of sight, I threw my last smooth rock so hard that my elbow hurt, like it sometimes did at recess when I aimed a softball from deep center field toward home plate.

It was a good throw, and the rock danced on the hard road clear to the turn and right on over the edge, clattering on the boards covering the spring.

three

Saturday I woke up feeling good until I remembered what lay before us. As I dressed, I heard kitchen sounds. "How'd you sleep, Jamie?" Mom asked when I came out of my room.

"Like a dead man. Didn't move once." It sometimes took me a long time to get to sleep, but last night the cool pillow never got warm under my cheek before I was gone.

"Me neither. I'm sore this morning, though," she said, rubbing her shoulder. "Chasing fire up and down hills like a runaway colt isn't good for an old woman. Better sit down and eat."

I smiled. She wasn't old. "Where's Dad?" I asked.

"Chores. He already ate, and he'll be ready to get started on the fence as soon as he comes in. It'll be a hot one again today."

Dad came in while I was finishing eating. I looked up at him, hoping against hope that he'd say we didn't have to do this job.

After breakfast, we got the tools and started around front to the truck. I knew we'd first have to go to town, and I wondered if Dad would insist we buy five posts when only two were needed, if that many. Whatever he decided, I knew I'd owe him for them; it was my fire, after all.

Dad stopped to turn on the hose and set the sprinkler in a corner of the lawn. It ran almost constantly in this heat. I was putting shovels, hammers, and a pick in the bed of the truck when my eye caught a glimpse of something on the ground. I set the tools down and went around behind for a better look. It was a sight I couldn't figure out for a minute.

"Dad!" I called. "Dad, come look at this."

"What is it, Jamie, a snake?" Dad started over. "Grab a shovel. Or call Keno." Keno loved to tangle with snakes, shaking and tossing them high in the air with his teeth.

I didn't say a word while Dad came up, but I'd figured it out by then. When he was beside me, he stopped and stared. "Well, I'll be tarred and feathered, inside and out."

He put his elbow on my shoulder and kind of leaned into me. "I thought I heard that truck this morning, before daylight. It goes to show, Jamie, you can't ever tell about people."

There, dumped on the ground behind the pickup, where we'd be sure to see them, were some posts. They were weathered, like those in Arlie's stack up by the spring. And most amazing of all, there were only two of them.

It was about eleven by the sun and already hotter than blue blazes when Dad and I finally finished setting the posts. Even with only two of them to do, the job was taking too long for me. My stomach was telling me it had been a long time since breakfast.

It was slow going in the rocky ground, and even through work gloves, yesterday's blisters made themselves known when I used the pick or the shovel. Dad took pains, as he always did when we worked on a job together, to teach me how to do it right. I tried hard to keep up with him, but he could outwork me any day. It wasn't clear to me how he did it, except he was always calm and in control, and never one to waste a motion.

His careful methods required the posts to be seated just as well as we'd build our own fence, just as if this fence had a right to be here.

I was splashing cool creek water on my neck and face when Keno surprised us by poking his head over the edge of the road bank. He'd ridden up with us earlier but trotted back home when he got hot and bored. Now he was back, and right behind him was Jerry.

"Hi, men. Working for the Leepers today, I hear." Jerry had a smart mouth most of the time.

"What are you doing here?" I asked. "So soon, I mean. I thought you weren't coming till after lunch."

"Mom brought me over early because she'll be busy at the store this afternoon. Lazy Nila's not coming in." Nila was a girl who worked—when she felt like it—in the grocery store Jerry's folks ran in town. "Aunt Evy told me you were up here enjoying yourselves."

I snorted, then decided to go along. "Absolutely!" I said. "More fun here than swallowing razor blades."

Jerry laughed at that, then slid on his feet down the bank and crossed the creek. Keno lay down again on the edge of the road and watched us apathetically, like he was trying to figure out what kind of strange creatures we were that we didn't have a better use for a hot summer morning than digging and hammering and sweating.

"Mom says hi," Jerry said to Dad. My Aunt Lois was Dad's next older sister.

"She didn't stop to help? I ought to throw her out of my will," Dad said.

Jerry took that as his prompt to help us himself. He grabbed a crowbar and helped Dad tighten the wires while I hammered in the big staples. At nearly sixteen, he had strong arms. Of course, he wanted to know all about what had happened. So while we worked, I told him the whole story—starting with the fire, right on through to the visit with Arlie Leeper on the road last evening, and ending with finding the posts this morning. He was as amazed as we had been about that part. He was one of the main Leeper-baiters at school, and he had no use for any of them.

"Must be a trick. These posts are probably poison to the touch," he said, "and we'll all swell up, turn purple, and explode."

I laughed, and Dad chuckled.

When we had the wires taut, we crossed the creek

and loaded the tools into the truck. Jerry and I climbed in the back with Keno for the short ride to the house. We stood, leaning on the cab, to get the wind on our sweaty skin.

"You watch," Jerry said suddenly.

"Watch what?"

"Arlie Leeper gave you those two posts, but you haven't heard the last of him." His voice was hard, and for Jerry, he looked very serious.

"What do you mean, Wise One?" I asked.

He shook his head sharply. "When Arlie Leeper gives something away, it's like a bee giving away its sting." He grinned at that, then got serious again. "You watch."

"I'll do that." I hoped he was wrong, but I didn't say so. Jerry always liked the last word.

We put away the tools. In the house, lunch was ready and we all sat down to it. Fried chicken, potatoes, corn on the cob, salad from the garden—it was the kind of big meal Mom usually fixed for Saturday noon, because Dad was home. I was starved and it was delicious. My mom was the best cook I knew.

When we stood up from the table, Mom asked us to take some table scraps to the pigs. While we were out there, Jerry looked over the burn area and asked more questions. It was starting to make a good story, even if I couldn't tell it the way Mom could.

"Want some currants?" I asked, to see Jerry's reaction. We were standing beside the big wild-currant bush that grew between the pigpen and the road. Jerry knew I was teasing. Not only was it too late in the year for currants, but we both knew that Jerry couldn't stand them—not since the time three or four years back when he'd gorged himself from this same bush and got sick in the night.

Jerry took a stick and poked the resting pigs through the fence. They didn't act like they minded—they just grunted and lay still. And when he scratched them around the neck, they seemed to positively enjoy it. They were fattening well, and this fall one would be butchered and the other two sold.

Suddenly, I saw a movement up on the Branagan road. It was a bicycle. "Look," I said. "Here comes Dennis!"

"Quick!" Jerry ducked down and ran across the road. "Under the bridge." I scampered after him.

We barely made it out of sight under the creek bridge when Dennis came around the curve where the Branagan road met ours. "Let's scare that little twerplet good," Jerry whispered. "Halloween noises, okay? Halloween noises."

We could see up through the cracks between the planks, and when Dennis hit the bridge, we let out the loudest and eeriest wails we could, like dying or suffering things.

Dennis jerked his handlebars like he'd been shot and nearly fell over into the creek bottom. It would have killed him for sure. But he recovered and started pedaling as fast as his old bike would let him.

He cleared the small rise in the road by our mailbox without looking back, pedaling like his tail was on fire. Then Jerry said, "Come on," and we hurried out from under the bridge and ran up by the mailbox so we could see down the road.

"Dennis!" Jerry screamed at the top of his lungs. Then, to me, he said, "Here. Fall down." We lay down quickly, halfway in the road, and pretended to be dead. But we positioned ourselves so we could watch. By the time Dennis stopped, he was almost down to the stand of brush on the hill where Mom and I had finally stopped the fire. He got off his bike and looked back uncertainly. We didn't move. After a long time, he started pedaling slowly back. "Look at him," Jerry muttered. "That kid doesn't have the sense God gave a goose."

I didn't have to look at him. Even out of half-open eyes, I knew well enough what Dennis Leeper looked like, his pale, pimply face usually streaked with dirt and his mouth always set in a silly half-grin. His thick glasses, their taped and rickety frames a miracle of endurance, were constantly slipping down his nose. I could see in my mind the frequent, awkward movement he made with the back of his hand to push them back into place, with no lasting effect except for the permanent smudge left by his knuckle on the lenses.

Seeing him pedal closer reminded me of the many

times over the summer when he'd pedaled his old bike slowly past the house, gawking to try to spot me. I tried to make sure he didn't. Otherwise, he'd follow me around all day like a sick puppy. At school, he would tag along with you until you about went crazy. Mostly, you learned to pretend he wasn't there at all. It wasn't nice, but you had to do it.

"He might not even see us if we don't move," Jerry said quietly. "He's blind as a drowned angleworm. He couldn't find the outhouse with a flashlight at noonday."

While Dennis was coming back, Jerry said to me, "Whatever you do, don't mention the raft, or we'll never get rid of him."

"Don't worry," I said.

Dennis pedaled up the rise, looking toward the yard, where he assumed we were. His face looked even paler than usual, and I could hear him breathing hard. He glanced our way, but he was nearly past before he saw us. He stomped on his brakes and skidded to a stop, almost falling over.

"Jamie?" he said tentatively. "Jerry?"

He stared another whole minute, I swear. Meanwhile, Jerry was starting to breathe faster, and I knew he was trying to cover a laugh. Suddenly, when he could stand it no longer, he sprang up and screamed at the top of his lungs, "Run for your lives! Pirates! Assassins! Murderers!"

Dennis fell sideways off his bike in the road. It didn't hurt him any, and we laughed while he got up slowly.

"What did you think, Leep?" Jerry asked. "That we both just collapsed here on the ground? Died of old age? Been scalped by Comanches? What were you going to do, stare at us until we resurrected and spirited over and grabbed you by the neck?" At that, Jerry lunged for Dennis, as if to choke him, but he didn't follow through. It still startled Dennis, though, and he stepped back and almost fell again.

But in a moment, to join the fun, Dennis's face crinkled clear up under his glasses into his cautious and hopeful grin. He'd go along with anything. He was the kind of kid who, if you told him to pick up a rattlesnake, would probably ask you which hand to use and which pocket to put it in.

Dennis was the most teased Leeper of them all. The most pitiful thing he regularly endured was what people called him. When he first moved here, one of the schoolteachers, glancing through the list of new Leeper names, accidentally read his name as "Denise." From that time on, when kids wanted to tease him, they'd call him that.

It made him wild at first and he'd screech, "I'm not a girl! I'm not a girl!" He would get fighting mad, but he wouldn't fight, since he was as meek as his dad was loud. After a while, though, he didn't get upset about it anymore and would even answer to the name.

My mom said it was sad that Dennis wanted friends so badly that he'd even let people call him a girl's name. She tried to get me to treat him in a Christian way, even if I didn't want him as a friend. She told me once, "The boy we know will grow and change, and what he turns into, in this life or the next, we all had a hand in creating." Mom liked to say things like that.

It made me think, and I'd only joined in actually taunting him once. Dennis was wearing an ugly hat at recess one cold day and somebody grabbed it and threw it to somebody else. Pretty soon, there was a circle of boys each holding the hat out toward him, then tossing it from one to another while Dennis scrambled pathetically to try to get it. It came to me and I tossed it on, but I glimpsed Dennis's eyes, frantic and hurt, looking beseechingly from one to another of us. I waited until the hat came back to me, then purposely made a poor toss—and tried to make it look accidental—so he could get it. He picked up the hat and looked up at me like he knew what I'd done, but I looked quickly away. I didn't want his thanks, but I didn't tease him again, either.

I didn't call him Denise and didn't actively tease him, but my Christianity could go only so far. I didn't like him around and I wouldn't pretend to. I mostly tried to ignore him, hoping he'd go away.

"What's the hurry, Denise?" Jerry asked in his adult voice. "You were really puttin' on the steam when you went past here."

"Just hurryin'." He was breathing hard.

"Such speed for a little lad. Almost looked like you were scared of something."

"Thought I heard a sound," Dennis answered with a trace of his silly grin. "Did you hear it?" he asked tentatively.

"Sound? What sound?" Jerry asked innocently.

"I don't know," Dennis said.

"Like what?" Jerry asked.

"Don't know. Screamin' or something."

"Screamin'? Holy mosquitoes! What are you talking about, screamin'?" Jerry pressed.

"Under the bridge."

"Under the bridge?" Jerry feigned surprise. "Screaming under the bridge? Why, Jamie," he looked at me, "doesn't Denise here know about the bridge?"

I shrugged to go along, since I didn't have the least idea where Jerry was headed with this.

Jerry turned back to Dennis. "You don't *know*, living up the road and crossing that bridge as often as you do?" He appeared dreadfully earnest for Jerry. He dropped his voice. "Fact is, Denise, there's things under that bridge would as soon kill and eat you as look at you."

Dennis glanced sideways toward the bridge. I couldn't tell if he was buying it all, but he wasn't rejecting it fully, either.

"Don't you worry, though. They never come out to prowl around the yard or anything. They just stay under that old bridge the whole time—waiting for the right meal to come along," Jerry went on. " 'Course, there is one other thing you need to know . . ."

"What?" Dennis asked quickly.

Jerry glanced around like he was telling a great secret he didn't want overheard. "Why, the reason them filthy monsters never bother Jamie or me. Not if we walk across that bridge a hundred and fifty-seven times a day."

Jerry waited until Dennis asked, "Why's that?" Then he answered slowly, pronouncing each word precisely and deliberately, in cadence, like a poem. "They don't bother us, my dear Denise, because what they love to eat is rusty bikes, broken-frame glasses, greasy, never-scrubbed faces, and ears so filled with dirt that with a little rain, they could grow fat, purple, prize-winning, blue-ribbon onions straight out the side."

It was an absolute production, the way Jerry recited it. But Dennis showed no reaction.

"That's why," Jerry concluded, leaning forward, his voice soft and calm and seemingly friendly, "that's why those wicked, vile creatures under the bridge only wait for *Leepers* to come by. See? That's why we call 'em *Leeper-eaters*!"

Jerry acted like a teacher merely passing on facts about the food chain in the oceans or how many bushels of bugs a seagull eats in a year. It took a bit for Dennis to see where he'd been led, then his eyes looked surprised, and maybe a little sad. But shortly, he made his simpering grin again, like he always did, and that was that.

We'd laughed enough at Dennis, so I asked him

where he was headed. He hesitated, not wanting to say he'd come to look for me, I figured, which he did so often. "Just . . . just . . . to see the fire."

"What fire?" Jerry asked. "There's no fire around here. You see any fire, Jamie?"

"Where it was. To see where the fire was yesterday. Right there." He pointed to the hill.

"Oh, *that* fire! Well, now you've seen it," Jerry said.

"And to walk the flume," Dennis added.

"Walk the flume?" Jerry asked, surprised. "The flume? I suppose you more properly mean *the aqueduct*?"

Jerry was laying it on now like an English teacher. *Nobody* called the flume an *aqueduct*.

"Why, gadfreys, man, walking the flume is a dangerous activity for such a young'un as you, Denise. You could fall right off and bust your head wide open."

"Yeah," Dennis said lamely.

"So maybe we'll have to show you how it's done," Jerry laughed.

"Oh, great," Dennis exclaimed, looking excited.

I couldn't believe Jerry had invited us to go along, especially since we were so anxious to work on the raft. If Dennis wanted to walk the flume, let him go ahead and walk it. But I knew Jerry loved to climb the flume as much as I did, and I figured he saw it as a good chance to taunt Dennis some more.

"Let's go, then," Jerry said as he strode off down the road. Jerry did like to be in charge.

Dennis left his dilapidated bike leaning against our

front locust tree and we started off down the road. Keno started to follow, but I sent him home. He'd have turned back anyway when we started up the hill. Climbing was too much work for him.

On the way, Jerry teased as usual. With enough time, he could usually get a rise out of Dennis about some subject or another for a minute or two before he'd slip back to his dull, compliant self. It was hard to get much out of him today, though—probably because he felt so glad to be included that he didn't dare to squawk.

"*Alla-malla, poko feetu?*" Jerry asked me suddenly.

I looked at him, then said, "*Nasoo lango.*"

It was a silly language game Jerry and I used to play when we were young—making up silly sounds for the fun of it and turning them, by inflection and emphasis, elaborate facial expressions and hand gestures, into questions and answers, orders and exclamations.

"*Fee-fuli masto tow-angus say foo-foo?*" Jerry asked.

"*Largo poni-walla exto povanitoo.*"

"*Waga-wago!*" Jerry pointed a finger at Dennis and said to me, behind his other hand but in a stage whisper, so Dennis would be sure to hear, "*Palu alotay. Sofi nanga?*"

"*Yotay,*" I answered.

"*Yotay-nanagan?*" Jerry opened his eyes wide like he was hearing something incredible and outlandish about Dennis, then added, "*Solay mata manga mutee!*" He laughed wildly.

Jerry was using the language game to make fun of Dennis. Dennis looked at us with his dumb grin, like he understood every word, and asked no questions. I thought of what Mom had said about his being willing to go along with any kind of treatment just to be included.

"Up here," Jerry commanded, just past where the fire had stopped. Climbing straight up was hard going. Jerry was in the lead, with me next, and neither of us wanted to be the first to stop to rest. Dennis was slow. At the ditch bank, we sat down to wait for Dennis in almost the same spot where Mom and I had sat yesterday after putting out the fire. Neither of us had much breath for talking while we waited, and it was hot.

As soon as Dennis caught up and started to sit down, Jerry asked, "Ready to go back?"

"No," he gasped.

"Let's go on, then." Jerry quickly stood and started down the bank. Dennis had no chance to rest.

Soon we were there.

"Well, here we are. You're here to walk the flume," Jerry said as he swept his hand outward in a grand gesture toward the big pipe. "And we're here to watch. Let's see what you can do, *Mister* Leeper, grand champion flume-walker supreme."

Dennis didn't move. His lungs were still recovering from the climb.

The flume was a grand structure. I shuddered to think that my fire might have burned it down. From the road it looked like a railroad bridge on the side of the hill. Heavy wooden beams rose up out of the ground and supported a corrugated pipe two and a half or three feet in diameter. The pipe carried the water of the big ditch fifty feet or more past a precipitous slide area full of loose shale and jagged rock ledges.

Dennis still stood staring. "Ever been up here before?" I asked him.

"Not really."

" 'Not really,' " Jerry mimicked. "That's what I thought."

Walking on the support beams was easy, because the footing was good and you could lean one hand against the pipe. Walking on the pipe itself was another matter. I didn't mind climbing up to sit astraddle it, but I'd never walked on it. Being so high above the cliff face bothered me. That was for daredevils like Jerry, who was already up on the pipe, walking right down the middle.

Jerry stopped and turned around. "What *is* the problem, my little man?" he called to Dennis, who still stood at the head of the pipe with his hands fidgeting. "You're here to walk the flume, aren't you? So let's get to walking." Jerry turned to me and said with a snort, pointing at Dennis, *"Pooty atra sissy-sissy!"*

Finally, Dennis stepped carefully out onto the wood behind me, keeping his eyes on his feet and pressing both hands against the pipe. He kept stopping to look down at the rocks below.

He edged toward me and I moved on. When I reached the other end, I looked back and could see he hadn't come very far, but that he was gaining confidence.

In the next few minutes, we all went back and forth two or three times. By now, Jerry was in grand form. He showed us that he could walk the pipe backwards and sideways. I wouldn't have been surprised if he'd put on a blindfold and done a few somersaults and a handstand or two.

"Why don't you young'uns get on up here?" he taunted. "What are you waiting for? Christmas? New Year's? A new Easter bonnet?"

Finally, for the first time in my life, I stood up on the pipe and walked a few feet to show Jerry or myself or someone that I could. I was glad I did it. But I was glad to sit down again, too, toward one end and look out across the road at the wide Payette.

I liked to watch the river. We weren't far from the first irrigation dam, and I could faintly hear the deep roar of the falls over it and see the white foam below. Out over the river, level with my eyes, several swallows darted and made sharp swerves and turns like they were playing tag in the bright afternoon sun. I watched them for a few minutes when suddenly they turned as one and flew quickly away downriver. Then I noticed why.

High over the north pasture circled the big hawk I'd watched all summer, out for a hunt. I marveled at how easily he rode the still air, always the patient hunter, watching and waiting. On the flume, we were half as high as he was.

Since he'd already got me to stand up on the pipe, Jerry went after Dennis, calling him a girl, a baby, a baby girl—until he finally climbed up on it, too. But he only sat astraddle it; he wouldn't stand up. He looked pleased with himself, sitting there, even though he didn't much look at ease. He kept his eyes mostly on the pipe in front of him, like it was a wild, bucking horse that might throw him off at any moment.

After a while, we got down off the pipe, Dennis and I at the downstream end and Jerry at the head. Jerry floated stalks of grass and small sticks through it and we all guessed at how many seconds it would take them to come out the other end. This gave Jerry an idea.

"I wonder if a person could float through here," he called as he bent down and squinted into the pipe.

"Not me, that's for sure," I answered. No obstructions were visible, although a slight curve kept us from seeing all the way through. But the idea of going through a black tunnel half filled with water, one that I couldn't see the end of, interested me about as much as a case of the mumps.

"Denise, you're the littlest. Come over here. Let's send you through, chile," Jerry called. Dennis stiffened beside me and shook his head.

Jerry's voice echoed through the pipe, low and

enticing, like the announcer's voice on a radio mystery show. "What say, Denise? You ready to become an explorer—to venture forth to places where man has never been? Think of it! You'd be a hero! Why, people would build monuments to you. They'd praise you far and wide for going down this dark tunnel. You'd be the first and only Leeper to go down in history!" And he laughed wickedly, like Dennis being a hero was the world's prizewinningest outrageous idea.

I glanced at Dennis and he had a faraway look in his eyes. Was he thinking about it? Then he suddenly shook his head vigorously and his face clouded over like he'd seen a ghost.

"No. Don't wanna go in there. No." He said it only loud enough for me. He backed a few paces away, his eyes big and scared, like he was ready to run for it.

"Oh, settle down, for heaven's sake," I told him. "Nobody's going to make you." I called, "Jerry, nobody wants to float through this thing. Let's throw rocks."

From this high up, to get a rock clear across the road and trees, so you could actually see it splash in the river, took a hard throw. Jerry made it every time, I made it most times, with the right size rock, and Dennis never made it. But he cheered every time either of us did. Once, after one of my best throws, he said quietly to me, "Wish I could throw like that."

I looked at his scrawny arms and figured he never would.

"Here, try this one." I gave him a smooth rock I'd

been saving for my last throw. It was the size of a small hen's egg, perfect for throwing. He threw with all his might, almost tumbling off the ditch bank with the effort, but he still didn't clear the road.

When we tired of throwing, Dennis said, "Got to get home. My dad'll be needin' me."

I was ready to go anyway. Jerry was on his way across the pipe toward us. "Dennis is ready to go home," I called to him. "It's hot up here."

"Good idea," he said. "Let's go down the rocks."

"Too steep," Dennis protested.

"Maybe for sissies," Jerry said, and started off. I went next, and Dennis followed.

First, we climbed down the support pilings to the slide area. By staying toward one side and avoiding the rock ledges in the middle, it was easy going at first.

We stopped while Jerry kicked out a watermelon-sized boulder and gave it a push. It thundered down the slide, flew off a ledge, and burst like a bomb at the bottom, sending fragments clear across the road.

About halfway down, we came to a patch of shale that slid under our feet. Two or three times, we had to shout at Dennis, behind us, to stop sliding rocks into us. He finally waited to let us get farther ahead.

Jerry and I picked our way carefully as the slide got steeper and harder to navigate. We were close to the bottom when I glanced back and saw that Dennis had stopped. I thought he was overdoing it to give us so much clearance, but I didn't pay much attention. When we'd almost reached the road, I looked again, and he still hadn't moved. But now I could see what the problem was. He'd swung over too far to the middle of the slide and had come to a ledge he couldn't get over.

"What are you doing, Dennis?" I called. "You can't come down that way. There's a drop-off. Come over to the side where we went." I waited and watched, but he didn't move.

Jerry had kept moving and was now at the bottom. "Come on, Denise, so we can tell everybody that girls can too climb down cliffs," he shouted up past me. "Come on. Show us."

By the time I joined Jerry on the road, it was clear that Dennis wasn't going anywhere. He was paralyzed, his back against the hill, arms sprawled out, fingers dug into the dirt, his face white and his eyes shut.

"Look at him," Jerry said.

Dennis moved his feet, sliding down a few inches in the process, stirring up pebbles that plummeted ten or twelve feet over the drop-off and bounced off the sharp rocks below.

"He's slid down to where he can't get himself back up," I said. "And he's facing out. That will never work."

Jerry clucked his tongue and shook his head.

"What's happening, Dennis?" I called. "Can you move? Answer me."

No answer.

"Dennis, do you need help?" I shouted.

"Denise!" Jerry took over. "Wake up! This isn't nap time."

Still no answer, but Dennis's feet scrambled, more small stones tumbled down, and he slipped closer to the edge.

"I'm going up to see," I said.

"No," Jerry said firmly. "He has to answer first." He turned back to Dennis. "Hey, kid, we're going home now. If you don't want to be saved, hang there like a fly in a spiderweb. If you want help, say so. And say so now!" He waited a moment, then shrugged and started up the road.

Seeing the need wasn't enough for Jerry. He had to hear you beg, like when he used to sit on me and act like he was going to drool in my face. He wouldn't quit until I said uncle, and then said it a second time. It was Jerry at his bullying worst.

Finally, a high, weak voice above us said, "Help me."

"Well, for crying in the middle of the long black night! We're going to have to come up there and save you, is that it?" Jerry turned and trotted back to where I stood. "I'll get him," he said to me. He seemed almost eager, now that the terms were clear.

"Do you want me to come up, Jerry?" I asked.

"No, I can do it. There isn't room, anyway."

Dennis was in a bad spot, and I wasn't sure how Jerry would be able to help him. He'd slipped enough by now that he could go right on over the edge if he didn't just sit still and hold on. Every time he tried to move his feet, he slipped a little more.

"Hang on, Dennis; don't move! Jerry's almost up to you!" I shouted. No answer came from Dennis. "Do not move at all!" I yelled again.

I could see the fear, and I thought I knew how he felt. Once, I'd been in a big tree beside the creek when I thought I couldn't go up or down. I finally made it down because no one else was around to save me and I had no choice, unless I wanted to stay perched there until the crows picked my bones clean. When we have to, we do more than we imagine we can. But it was a bad feeling, and my legs were shaking when I came down.

Jerry was off to the side of Dennis now, looking things over. He'd stopped his taunting. He slowly worked his way closer.

"Now, listen to me, Dennis," Jerry said. Jerry was all business now, and I knew he was concentrating hard if he forgot to say Denise. "I'm gonna move over a little more, see, but I can't get clear over to where you are. No, there isn't room for both of us to plant our feet. So listen, when I say the word—after I get my feet set—you give me your hand. But don't move. Don't move your feet yet, but just your hand when I say to. We'll start with that."

No answer.

"Okay? Do you hear me? Can you do it?"

No answer.

Jerry moved over and, when he got his feet planted, said, "Okay. Now."

No movement.

Jerry told him again, waited, and finally reached over and grabbed Dennis's wrist. At this, Dennis came alive. His feet started scrabbling, and his other hand reached over and frantically grabbed Jerry's arm, the way a drowning man would lock onto a log floating by.

It caught Jerry off guard. "Stop it, Leep!" he shouted. "Good night! Stop it, you idiot! You'll pull us both down!"

Jerry shoved Dennis back against the rocks and kind of shook him a couple of times. This slowed down the turmoil his feet were making, but he didn't let go of his grip.

"Criminy, man! You'll kill us both!" Jerry shouted. "Now, you do what I tell you. Do you hear me, Dennis? You do what I tell you! Or so help me, I'm going to leave you right here till these hills crumble to dust and the buzzards come for you!"

You could have heard the last part clear across the river.

I guess Jerry got through to him because Dennis nodded quickly. He appeared to be cooperating more now as Jerry told him where and when and how to place each hand and foot. As soon as he did that, the crisis was over.

In a minute, they'd moved away from the drop-off and were safely back into the loose shale. Jerry tried to shake Dennis off and finally had to reach over and pry his fingers loose from his forearm, like he was picking cockleburs off his sleeve.

Jerry came down first, shaking his head, leaving Dennis to make his slow and wobbly way. At the road, Jerry puffed his cheeks and let out a big breath while he rubbed at the bright red finger marks on his arm. "Man, I tell you," he said. *Maybe even Jerry had been scared for a moment,* I thought, *when Dennis sank his claws into him and threatened to pull them both down.*

We watched Dennis come down the rest of the way like an old man, weak and hobbling, his face pale and drawn. Without a word, we started up the road toward home, Dennis at the rear. I glanced back at him once. There were tear streaks under his glasses.

four

When we got back from the slide, Dennis started home immediately. As he was pulling away on his bike, his dad's beat-up old truck came along from the direction of town. Arlie shouted something at him, then drove on toward home, leaving Dennis to pedal in the dust behind him.

Jerry shook his head and said, "Even his own dad doesn't like him." It made me hurt some for Dennis. What must it be like to have a man like Arlie Leeper for a dad?

We drank from the hose and lay in the shade in the yard awhile with Keno. It was hot, and it felt good to lie still in the cool grass.

When we'd rested, we got up and headed for the raft site.

"A pretty good collection of supplies here, cousin lad," Jerry intoned when he looked at the logs I'd gathered behind the woodshed, "but I don't think these will quite do. No, not quite." He was speaking in the exaggerated and mocking adult tone he used for effect. He did it a lot, when no grown-ups were around, to be a comedian and to sound like the boss.

Jerry always made himself the boss of any project, no matter what it was. And I generally gave him no argument. It was the way it had always been with Jerry and me. Jerry was good at a lot of things, but taking orders wasn't one of them.

At first, I hadn't wanted Jerry involved with my raft. Not only because he was bossy but also because he was good at ruining my things. Like breaking the only silver-tipped arrow in my bow-and-arrow set a few years back when he shot it at Palmer's old horse. It hit him harmlessly in the side, but when it fell under the spooked animal's hooves, it came out in two pieces. But I came to see that I needed help on the raft, and Jerry could be counted on.

"Does this thing float?" Jerry asked, kneeling beside the logs I'd put together.

"It's not bad," I said. "But it's too low in the water, and it's tippy. I don't trust . . ."

"What we need here is more buoyancy," Jerry interrupted as he stood and pondered the situation.

"Sure, Professor, but bigger logs are too hard to drag out," I protested. "And when they're water-logged, they're hard to saw or chop. Look at that one I started on last year." I pointed to a short, stout log I'd managed to get partially up onto the bank last summer. My saw mark was visible where I'd cut into it two or three inches before the saw jammed in the pulpy gray wood.

"Not what I had in mind, lad. Not at all," Jerry said. "Look." He pointed behind me. I turned. There was a bunch of silver metal cans stacked against the back of the woodshed. I hadn't seen them before.

"Look at these. Brought these with me this morning and hid 'em back here before I came up the creek to find you. What do you think of that?"

"I don't know what I think of it," I said. "Because I don't know what they are."

"They're from the store. Rice and stuff comes in 'em. See, we won't need bigger logs at all. A few more small ones and when we get some lift under it—like these cans will give us—she'll float. They've got good, tight lids, and if we tie some of them on underneath, we can ride high and dry as the Queen of Sheba down the Nile."

"That sounds good, Captain," I said, "if we can get them to stay on."

"We'll figure it out."

As we set about measuring and figuring, it came to me that this raft might really float, after all. It gave me a kind of shiver to think about it.

We worked like crazy through the rest of the hot afternoon, sawing and hammering, adding to the framework I'd already put together. It looked like we might get done today.

We had the frame the way we wanted it and were taking a break in the shade of the riverside brush when Mom showed up with Dad right behind her. They had grape Kool-Aid with ice cubes for us, which we gulped down. It hurt my throat, it was so cold and sweet.

"Supper in twenty minutes," Mom said, and they went back to the house.

The Kool-Aid broke our momentum, and we lounged until suppertime. It felt good to sit down and cool off a little. We rubbed the ice cubes on our wrists.

We were halfway through supper when Mom asked, "You boys are serious about this raft, aren't you?"

"I guess so," I said. "We've got it all planned. I've worked on it for a long time, you know." She shook her head and didn't say anything.

"Not like you're working today," Dad said.

"We might get 'er in the water today," Jerry said.

"I don't like it," Mom said. "It's dangerous."

She was worried, and I understood why. Stories persisted in our valley of those the river had claimed over the years, and my parents made sure Marie and I were reminded of them regularly.

Speed McCallister, a man a little older than Dad, was known as a strong swimmer, but when fishing with friends on the North Fork one day, he fell in and was swept away.

Old Arny Ganskin was the pond walker at the sawmill who fed the logs onto the chain that pulled them up to the saw. He had done his job for ages and could hop around on a pond full of bobbing, slippery logs all day long—in a raging blizzard, if he had to—like he was on a hardwood floor. But one day, unaccountably, he slipped and hit his head and went under. Nobody missed him until the logs stopped coming up the chain.

And there was husky Ralph Guthrie, barely twenty-one, who, with too much to drink at the town dance one summer night years back, took a dare to swim across the river. Out behind the old dance hall, where the stream starts its broad horseshoe bend around the town, he stripped down in the moonlight, waded out, and started off fine. His friends took his clothes and started for the other side to meet him downstream, stopping on the highway bridge to shine a car's spotlight on him. They watched in horror as he made it about three-quarters of the way across before he seemed to just give out and stop stroking, like he wanted to rest awhile. Facedown, he floated slowly under the bridge before sinking while his helpless buddies yelled and cursed and cried up above.

I knew these stories by heart. Because my parents were both non-swimmers and afraid of the water, they'd made it a point to scare Marie and me to keep us safe.

Dad went on, "You boys are making such progress, it's time I put in a word of caution." He looked at Jerry. "You know that Jamie here can't swim like you can." In spite of swimming lessons, I was never confident in the water. My swimming was more like sinking. Nearer to town, there were river shallows and the canal where Jerry and other town kids swam and dove in the summer. I never joined them. I liked to be near the river, but not in it.

"I know, Uncle Dale," Jerry said in the adult tone he

could put on anytime, but with surprise in his voice because of how serious Dad was. "There'll be no problem. I'll see to it." It sounded like he was reciting a pledge.

Dad said, "Of course, when you talk about going out on the raft, boys, you're not talking about a wild ride down the river, like Huck Finn down the Mississippi, are you?" He chuckled. "You just mean to float in the shallow water below the logjam, right?"

"Uh, yeah, that's right," I said, though I hadn't actually given any thought to it. Certainly we didn't plan to really *go* anywhere. Where could we go, especially with the dams downstream that would spill us if we tried to go over them?

"One thing I'm going to ask of you. That's to use a rope. One of you can stand on shore and hold the end while the other one is on the raft."

A rope? Jerry stopped eating and looked at me. It seemed to kind of take the fun out of rafting to be roped to shore.

Dad said, "I know you probably don't like the idea, boys, but the water here is just too stout, even near the shore. If you were to accidentally get out into the main stream . . ." He waved his hand in the direction of the river. "I just can't let you go out without being sure you're safe." He didn't pause for our response, but turned to me. "Jamie, there's rope in the granary and more in the barn. You know how to tie them together so they won't slip. Don't use my newer ones, but even without those, you can probably round up seventy or eighty feet."

"Okay," I agreed. It didn't sound too bad if we had eighty feet of leeway. Maybe if we did it Dad's way at first, we could get him to let us loose later.

Dad said, "Call me when you're ready to go out the first time."

"I wish we didn't live by this river at all," Mom said. It was hard for Mom to let things go.

"I want to ride," Marie said.

"We'll see," Mom said quickly.

My parents' soberness got me to thinking, and I remembered my own near-drowning. It was in the summer two years before, when I was twelve. Jerry had been here, and we were climbing around on the logjam, the big pile of debris—mostly runaway logs from several small sawmills way up the river and a few fallen trees— that lodged at the mouth of the creek below our house. Jerry would always go out farther than I would. He'd make a point of that.

It was early in the summer, and spring runoff was still high. The jam was scary then, with the logs wet and slippery and the dark water sucking menacingly around them. That made it all the more fun.

Jerry had wanted to throw a rock clear across the river—which I knew he couldn't do, even though his shoulders and arms had developed more than mine. I had a lighter build to start with, and although I had already passed him in height, it looked like I was likely to remain lanky and thin.

Even with his good throwing arm, Jerry couldn't

make it. The river was too wide. When the three forks came together up the canyon, they formed a powerful and tumultuous stream filled with dark whirlpools swirling around massive boulders. A quarter mile above the sawmill, the torrent raged in one final, steep rush of wild white water that I was always scared to look at when we crossed it on the silver highway bridge. After this last wild surge, the river entered our valley, tamed and widened but still deep and strong.

Jerry kept stepping out farther onto the jam, pausing now and then to fling one of the rocks he carried. I sat down on a log to watch. The farther out he went, the less stable the logs were and the more they rocked and bounced with his steps. Most people would have stopped by now, but Jerry wasn't like most people.

He'd made his way to a big Douglas fir on the outer edge of the jam whose crown had driven in under the other logs when it had roared in like a runaway torpedo a few weeks before, at the peak of high water. The roots still poked out into the stream, where they quivered and swayed under the constant pressure of the water tearing at them.

It was obvious that Jerry was going to try for those roots, the farthest point he could get to, to make his last throws. I didn't see how he could possibly make it, but he knew the chances of that as well as I did. And besides, you couldn't tell Jerry anything.

He did fine for the first few feet, where he could bend over and hold on to the sagging branches with their dead brown needles. But the lower trunk of a mature fir tree doesn't have any branches, and Jerry had a final fifteen feet or so to traverse with no handholds. He edged along sideways, floating his arms in the air for balance like he was conducting an orchestra.

I wouldn't have traded places with him for seven million dollars. Where the sodden bark was still attached, the trunk would be slippery enough. But when he came to a patch where a whole section of bark had been ripped away in the tumble down the river, the wet yellow-white wood looked as sheer and smooth as greased marble.

The bare patch was three or four feet long, and Jerry began sliding sideways an inch at a time—real slow, like a man being urged off a gangplank by little jabs of a sword to increase his interest in going.

Then he fell. One moment he was edging along in the middle of that slippery bare spot. The next he was making a hole in the water, seat first, downstream from the fir, without even time to yell. As he went under, the rocks he'd held in his hands came splashing down around his head like spent bullets.

As it turned out, Jerry popped right up and made it to shore by turning quickly into the quiet lee of the log-jam. He was a good swimmer.

I was the one with the problem.

Startled at seeing Jerry fall, I had jumped up without thinking. My foot slipped and I stepped into the gap between two logs. Instantly, I was under water and bumping my head and back on the tight logs above me. I panicked.

It couldn't have been more than a few seconds, but I knew I was going to die. Clawing frantically at the logs above me, I found no openings. I had drifted away from the gap I fell through and I didn't know which way to turn.

My lungs begged for air. Just as terror was about to overtake me completely, I suddenly found my head jerked above water. I heard my name over and over: "Jamie, Jamie, Jamie." It was Dad. He was in the water with me, holding me with one arm and holding a log with the other.

He'd seen it all and had run from the yard. He jumped instantly into the same hole I'd fallen into and pulled me up. For a long time after we pulled ourselves onto the logs, he held me against him, both of us shaking. Jerry stood nearby, shivering and quiet.

I wondered if I could have done what Dad had done if I was as scared of the water as he was. It took more than I had in me.

So, as to the river, my folks could be sure I'd be careful.

Now that I'd sat down at supper, I was tired. It had been a long day. If I'd been working alone, I would have quit for the day. But Jerry was full of energy, and when we got up from the table, he was on his way to find the ropes. I went out with him. When we'd gathered several sections, we laid them out on the ground and tied them together.

We paced them off to see how much length we had. Jerry didn't like my twenty-seven steps. "Too short," he said. He declared twenty-four to be the right number of yards.

Next, we set to figuring out how to get the cans tied on underneath. They were over a foot high and about nine by nine inches square. Since they were perfectly smooth, with no fastening points whatsoever, neither twine nor baling wire worked very well. We finally settled on both, lashing the cans to one another and then to the logs.

"Easy now," Jerry cautioned. Carefully, we turned the raft over, carried it the few steps to the water, and set it in gently right below the logjam.

"Thar she blows, matey!" Jerry said. We stood back and surveyed our vessel. It looked good. The cans sank to less than half their width, leaving the deck half a foot above water.

"Get the rope," Jerry ordered as he put first one foot and then the other onto the craft. It was exciting to see it still floating buoyantly, even with Jerry standing in the middle of it.

"First, I'll get Dad, Captain," I said. "Like he said." I trotted to the house and called Dad.

I went back and tossed Jerry one end of the line. He knelt and poked the end of it through a gap in the logs and tied it tight.

"Now the pole."

"Yes, Majesty." I handed him a long, smooth pole I had fished out of the river months back. He pushed off. I wrapped my end of the rope around a limb on a log. By then, Mom and Dad both were beside me, and Marie soon showed up.

"Hey!" Jerry called. "Feels great!"

Dad looked admiringly at our work. "Looks like a good job, Jamie," he said quietly. Mom didn't say a word.

I watched Jerry another minute, then said, "Let me try." It was my project to start with.

"Okay, come on." He poled back up to shore, stepped off, and took the rope. I crawled on carefully and sat down.

I poled downstream a ways. It was great. Here, below the logs, the river was so quiet and smooth you could skip BB's across it like rocks when you put the gun barrel flat on the surface of the water.

"Pretty good, huh?" Jerry asked.

We each took several more turns. Mom even let Jerry take Marie for a ride. She was scared at first, but settled down and loved it. Mom and Dad were offered turns but didn't accept. But they seemed to enjoy watching the rest of us.

It was close to dark when Dad said, "I think you'd best wrap it up for today, boys. Tomorrow's another day." I was tired enough that that sounded good to me. We pulled the raft in and lifted it onto the bank. It had been a good day, and it felt like the start of something big.

five

Sunday morning Jerry woke me up early. "Let's get to the raft," he said. He was already up and dressed. We hurried out. It was before seven, and Mom and Dad weren't up yet. It was their one day to sleep in. The morning was still and fine and not yet too hot.

On the raft, I felt safe as long as I could see the bottom or when the ten-foot pole sank to less than half its length, but anything else made me nervous. I felt I needed to overcome my fear, so when it was my turn, I pushed out just a little farther each time. It made me feel brave. Of course, Jerry always went out farther than I did, and in his hands the pole went down seven, eight, nine feet.

"I'm going way out this time," Jerry said on his fourth or fifth turn. He poled straight out toward the main river while I fed out the rope. Soon he had to kneel to reach the bottom with the pole. When he finally reached the point where he left the quiet water and the stream caught him, he sat down with the pole across his knees like an Indian with a giant peace pipe.

"Wahoo!" he shouted as he picked up speed and

sailed away from me, holding on to the logs under him. I was nervous just watching how fast he was going. The rope played out rapidly until it reached its last coil, then it jerked in my hands and jumped clear out of the water. It was a good thing I had it wrapped around a log. The raft spun around like a calf in a rodeo when it hits the end of the lasso at top speed. Finally, the craft steadied and began a slow swing toward shore at the end of its eighty-foot leash.

Back in the slow water, Jerry sat and let me tow him in.

"That was great!" he shouted when he was halfway back. "I'm going out again. Come on, come with me."

"Mmmm, I don't know," I said. "What about the rope?"

Jerry said, "It'll be fine if you tie it tight."

It seemed a little dangerous, but I'd worked all these years on the raft, and now it sounded silly to only go endlessly up and down in the same spot. I looked toward the house.

"Only if you don't go out so far," I said. I tied the rope tighter and climbed on.

As Jerry pushed us out, it was scary to see the pole going deeper and deeper, and already I was wishing I hadn't come. From this vantage point, the main river looked awfully fast and strong. As the corner of the raft met the current, Jerry pulled in his pole and sat with his back against mine. The raft bucked, and I looked for places to lock my fingers into cracks between the logs. I was scared. I knew if I fell off this thing, I'd have no chance.

As we picked up momentum and became one with the current, things smoothed out. I was facing upstream, watching the rope play out, and I braced myself as the last two or three coils on the shore rapidly snaked away into the water.

"Get ready!" I yelled. I felt Jerry hunker down. We were prepared, but when the taut rope sprang from the river like a lunging sea serpent, it was still a jolt.

Suddenly, we were awash in two or three inches of cold river. "Yow!" Jerry laughed as the water hit our legs and seats. Now, slanting to one side, we could only wait and hold on as we made our long arc toward shore. I didn't like it. I hoped the rope would hold.

"Hey," Jerry shouted. "Look at that! We're losing our cans!" I turned my head and saw what was happening. Under the pressure of the water when we hit the rope's end, three of our cans had broken loose and were floating away. So this was the reason for the slant and for our riding so low in the water.

"Man, there goes another one," Jerry called. He tried to reach for it, but that only tipped us more.

I didn't like that. "Lean this way!" I yelled. "Forget the cans, Jerry! You'll tip us over!" I lunged for the rope and held it. It made me feel better.

Cans continued to pop out—six in all, of the twelve we had under us. Gradually we stabilized, but we were much lower in the water.

Finally, in shallower water, Jerry helped bring us toward shore with the pole. I turned to watch the half-dozen escapees bob away, glinting in the morning sun like a family of silver geese out for a swim.

"Man, what a ride!" Jerry exclaimed. He liked anything crazy.

We towed ourselves back upstream with the rope, then pulled the raft onto the bank and turned it upside down. All the remaining cans were loose. Once the first one had popped out, the twine and wire had slackened, setting others free.

"We have more design work to do," Jerry said as we studied the problem.

"Either that or we stay in calm water from now on, like we're supposed to, Screwball," I said.

Jerry gave me one of his looks, like I was clearly a hopeless case.

I decided to do the chores. Dad always did morning chores, but I needed to pay him back for helping me with the posts yesterday morning.

Jerry helped me. Even though he had stronger arms and bigger hands, he wasn't used to milking, and I could beat him at it. He also hadn't learned to keep his face to the front to avoid the cow's quick, bristly tail. After a couple of good swats in the eyes, he declared that next time, so help him, he'd tear it out by the roots. So I decided to save the cow's life and I held the tail for him.

It was a slow day. After this morning's run, we needed more cans, and we couldn't fix the raft until we had them. We talked about better ways of keeping them on but didn't come up with any great ideas.

Church wouldn't start until two o'clock. The late start gave Pastor Soter time to hold morning services in his regular church in Boise, then drive the thirty miles to our town. Jerry and I couldn't decide whether we'd go today or not. I liked church and I especially liked Pastor Soter, and I went most of the time with Mom and Marie. Dad only went now and then.

By late morning, it was hot and sultry. Clouds in different shades of gray had built up until the sky was a cooking-pot lid sitting on top of us. A hot, burning breeze came through for a few minutes, making the heavy cottonwood leaves in the riverside trees clatter together. I thought a thunderstorm might whip up, but it soon became still again and even hotter than before.

Finally, to cool off, we retreated for a few minutes into what we called the cellar—our food storage house beside the woodshed—where foot-thick, sawdust-filled walls kept the temperature nearly the same all year round. We pulled the heavy door shut and soaked up the coolness, sitting on the floor beside the freezer and the shelves of bottled fruit. Three or four watermelons from the garden lay cooling along one wall. Some were dark green and as round as basketballs, others long and striped, like green torpedoes. This time of year, we ate a melon most every day. The perfect ones split open with a snap when you barely pushed a blade into them. The less than perfect ones went to the pigs. With so many melons, we could afford to be fussy.

I reached up and swung the dangling bare light bulb back and forth to make monster shadows leap along the walls.

Jerry said, "Did I tell you who came by this morning? Before I woke you up?"

"No. Who? Oh, well, sure, I can guess that one. Dennis, I'd say."

"Yep. Dear Denise." He snickered. "When I woke up and went out, he was already out there by the front gate, sitting on that rusty contraption he calls a bike. Just sitting there like he was waiting for a streetcar."

"They don't run here anymore," I joked. "What did he say? Did you talk to him?"

"Said he came by to see what we were doing today. I told him you were sleeping, that's what you were doing, and I stared at him till he left. We sure don't want him to know we're building a raft," Jerry said seriously, "or he'll be down here every day, driving us crazy."

"Dad would probably want us to invite him," I said.

Jerry said "Hmph. And the Queen wants her colonies back, too." He laughed. "When did he tell you this?"

"Oh, he's always trying to get me to spend time with Dennis. Mom, too. They say he's lonely."

"Now, that's a ponder—that a Leeper should be

lonely, what with their extreme sociability and all," Jerry sneered.

"Dad's always telling me I ought to get to know him better."

"Sure! That's what I want most in life—to get to know a Leeper, right down deep in his puny, little heart." Jerry laughed.

After a moment, he said, "I tell you what we could do, though." He waited for me to look at him. "If he wants to go rafting with us, we could put old Denise on that raft and give it a big shove downriver." We both laughed at that.

We'd had a quick lunch and had helped Mom clean it up when she said it was time to get ready for church. By then, Jerry and I had decided it was too hot to bother. Dad would drop off Mom and Marie and go visit his dad while he waited an hour to pick them up. We asked him to stop and pick up more cans behind the store while he was in town.

After everybody left, there wasn't much to do. It would have been better to have gone to church. I always felt good afterward. But today we'd made a different choice. We went back outside and wandered around awhile—over to the creek, then out to the north pasture, where the cow raised her head and kept her eye on us. We climbed for a while on the logjam, but the heat kept us from staying long. Our talk was aimless—first of tree houses and calf riding and rabbit shooting and fishing, then of school starting and Jerry's advice about high school and girls, on both of which subjects he considered himself a great expert.

Finally, we sat in the shade of the brush and tossed rocks into the river. When it was about time for everybody to come home, we went to the yard to get a drink from the hose, and there came Dennis coasting down the road into our parking area, like he'd been watching for us.

"Man, can't we ever get rid of this kid?" Jerry exclaimed.

"Here come Mom and Dad, too," I said. The white Dodge had appeared at the curve down by the Big Ranch.

"Better get that wore-out old bike out of the way!" Jerry called to Dennis. " 'Course, it looks like it's been run over a couple of times already, doesn't it?"

I thought it might be good, before we sent him home, to have Dad and Mom see that we were spending time with him.

Our car pulled in. Dad and Mom both spoke to Dennis as they got out. To me, Dad said, "I got the . . ."

"Thanks, Dad," I said, cutting him off, hoping he wouldn't mention the cans. "We were just about to start the chores."

Dad looked surprised, but I guess he got the idea. He said, "Okay," and he and Mom headed for the house.

Marie was slow getting out of the car and she was the one who spilled it. "Dad got cans, Jamie," she said. "For the raft. In the trunk."

"Yeah, okay," Jerry said to her quickly. "You go on in now. We . . ."

"Raft?" Dennis asked. "You have a raft?" He looked right at me. Jerry gave a small groan and rolled his eyes upwards.

"Well, we're sort of building one," I said quietly.

"You are?"

He stood looking at me like a little kid before Santa Claus, but he was still holding his bike and already half turned to go, like he had no hope. I was opening my mouth to say something inviting, because I didn't know how not to, when Jerry said, "We've got chores now. You go." Jerry was a lot tougher than me.

No one said anything more while Dennis climbed on his bike and wobbled away. Jerry shook his head. "Blast! Now we'll never get rid of him as long as we live," he said.

six

We didn't work on the raft after Dennis left because it was Sunday, a day of rest, when our family only did necessary chores. When I woke up Monday morning, my first thought was of having to hoe. Since I hadn't finished the weeding last week, I'd have to work on it even when Jerry was here. That was the deal my parents had made with me. Jerry said he'd help. We had breakfast with Dad before he left for work, to get an early start. And we'd purposely gone to bed early last night.

At the garden, a green oasis in the middle of a black expanse, we talked about hiding out from Dennis, but we decided it wouldn't do any good. Maybe if we hurried, Jerry thought, we could manage to be out on the water before he came by. But it wasn't to be.

Dennis showed up long before the sun came over the big hill and hit the garden.

We saw to it that he hoed his share to pay his way. He was unusually talkative and excited, full of questions about the raft, until he just about drove us crazy, like we knew he would. Jerry finally sent him to the far east side, in the potatoes, and kept the two of us on the west, in the cucumbers and pole beans, with several rows of late corn in between.

About ten o'clock, Arlie's old truck came down the road and turned toward town. "Hey, Denise, there goes your dad!" Jerry yelled. "He probably needs you for something." To me, he added, "I hope, I hope."

"Shhhhh," Dennis said. He quickly crouched down behind the corn.

"What's that mean, anyway?" I asked Jerry.

"Danged if I know," he said. The truck passed by without a glance our way from Arlie, and Dennis slowly stood up.

"What's the problem? Why are you so worried about your dad?" I called.

"Don't know."

"Is he looking for you?"

"Don't know."

" 'Don't know, don't know,' " Jerry said. "Hey, Buckshot, what else can you say?"

Dennis came around from behind the corn. "He wouldn't want me down here," he said. "My dad wouldn't."

"And why not?"

"Don't know." Jerry and I looked at each other in amazement, and Dennis added, "He's probably got work for me. And he doesn't like me down here all the time."

Jerry picked up on that idea right away. "Oh, so you're

too good for other people, is that it?" he asked mockingly. "You fine Leepers are a cut above other folks?"

"No, no," Dennis said weakly. "Not that."

"Maybe they're a branch of the royal family of Calcutta," Jerry snorted. "Or third cousins, only twice removed, of the exalted king of Gibraltar. Or maybe a teensy-weensy fragment of one of the Ten Lost Tribes. They probably have servants to carry them to the outhouse on cold mornings!" His voice had a satiric lilt to it. "Shall we prostrate ourselves in the dust now or later, Excellency?" He made a low bow toward Dennis, who smiled about it all.

Suddenly, Jerry was serious. "If your dad didn't want you to come, why did you, Leep?"

"Wanted to see the raft."

"To see the raft, to see the raft. Well, you keep that hoe moving, lad, and we'll let you know when it's time for that," Jerry replied sharply. Dennis immediately went back to his place and his hoe resumed its scraping on the dry ground.

Soon Mr. Skelton came by in his green Studebaker and put the mail in the box. I checked it, but there was only a bill from Idaho Power and Light and a renewal notice for *The Saturday Evening Post.* I took these to Mom the next time we went to the hose for a drink. I knew she was hoping for a letter from her dad in Arizona, but with arthritis in his hands he didn't write often.

In the late morning, we stopped to watch the train go up the tracks across the river, on the trip it made two or three times a week. It had eight empty flatcars today, some of which would be dropped off at the sawmill to be loaded with lumber.

After the engine passed, a trail of gray smoke floated in the calm morning air toward us and made it to about the middle of the river before dissipating. Watching the smoke and listening to the train's clacking rhythm put a spell on the three of us that made getting back to work difficult. It was hot now, and after our next trip to the yard to drink we didn't bother going back.

We lounged on the grass for a while and groaned about how hot it was.

Suddenly, Jerry stood up and said, "Beat you to the raft!"

He liked a head start. With that we were off. Of course he won, and Dennis was last. Just as I got there, I remembered the hoes and shovels we'd left in the garden and I went back to put them away. Dad liked his tools put away.

When I came back behind the woodshed, Dennis and Jerry were sitting on the stockpile of boards and small logs. Jerry had his shirt off. I heard him say, "Naw, too much work. Way too much work."

Dennis didn't say anything, so I asked, "What is?"

"Oh, this kid's harebrained idea to keep the cans on," Jerry answered.

"Which is?"

Dennis looked at Jerry like he had to get permission to answer, and when Jerry kind of waved his hand, finally said, "Tie them on, but build a wood frame around the outside, too. With these thin boards here. Like a trap."

"A trap. Too much work," Jerry protested again with another wave of his hand.

I sat down to think about it. It would take work all right, but nobody had a better idea. Finally, I said, "Sounds like it would work. Even if a can came loose, it couldn't float out of the frame."

Jerry looked at me and gave a quick nod. It was a good idea, and he knew it. But he wouldn't take it from a Leeper. Dennis beamed.

As soon as that was settled, Jerry took over again, telling us how to do the job, just like it was his idea.

We were making a good ruckus, sawing and hammering, when the sound of the noon mill whistle floated down the river. When I heard Mom call a few minutes later, I went to talk with her to see if we could postpone lunch a bit. We had such a good rhythm going, we'd be done soon.

The radio was on. Mom liked the soap operas, and I didn't mind some of them, either, whenever I was in the house. Helen Trent and Pepper Young seemed like friends after so many years, even though I didn't know what any of them looked like.

Mom already had lunch figured out. A picnic basket was ready, with sandwiches, potato chips, and a jar of cold Kool-Aid.

"How are you getting along with the Leeper boy?" Mom asked.

"Okay, I guess. He's helping."

"I'm glad."

She reminded me to be careful and I went out the door with the picnic basket. Dennis was mostly in the way, to tell the truth, but he had come up with a good idea about the cans and done a lot of weeding, so he'd earned his spot.

With three of us working, it wasn't long before the raft was in the water. And with the rope tied to the new frame underneath, we were ready to go.

We took the lunch and ate on board, tethered close to the logjam. The raft held the three of us just fine, though it didn't give us much room to move around. But the cans stayed in place and everything seemed good.

After lunch, Jerry and I took turns. Dennis was content to handle the line. After my turn, as I came back in, I handed him the pole. He looked at me, then grinned and scrambled on.

"Hey, let me off first, you madman!" I hollered as I leaped to the logjam. "You'll spill us! What's wrong with you?!" He'd scared me.

Jerry and I sat and watched him as he knelt and poled his way down the quiet channel. He was a little clumsy and wobbly, but he never stopped grinning.

When Dennis came back from his cautious turn, Jerry replaced him and poled a ways out into the current.

He wanted to see how the cans would hold under pressure, he said. I made a secure tie to a log.

Jerry rode downstream to the end of the rope and pulled himself back. "Let me try that again," he said as he swung back out. This time, though, instead of entering only the edge of the fast stream as he'd done before, he kept going, kneeling down and reaching into the water with his arms as the pole disappeared farther and farther into the depths. He pushed out as far as he could possibly go before sitting down for the ride.

"Where are you going, Admiral?" I called. He didn't answer but only waved as the current pulled him away. When he hit the end of the rope this time, the line sprang out of the water, vibrating like a huge guitar string and spraying fine droplets into the air. Jerry gave a shout and held on as the raft jerked hard and arced back toward shore. The cans held.

When Jerry pulled himself back up to us, he pronounced the vessel satisfactory. "As good as the *African Queen*," he said.

Over the next hour we all took turns, as many as we wanted. Jerry was the only one adventuresome enough to head out into the main stream, though. On my off time, I put away the hammers and other tools.

Mom and Marie came once to check on us. I took Marie for a long ride. She begged for more, but Mom said it was enough and that she'd get sunburned on the water and made her get off. We tried hard to talk Mom into a ride, but she wouldn't consider it. She cautioned us again to be careful and they both went back to the house. I knew she didn't know about Jerry actually getting out into the current.

It was hot and bright on the water. Jerry had his shirt back on, and Dennis's light arms and face were turning red. My face felt tight and my arms showed a narrow, pinkish band just above where my short sleeves met my tan.

"Let's get the dog on here," Jerry said after a while. "See how the old critter likes it." Keno was stretched out in the shade, watching us and dozing. I knew he would never come onto the logjam if I called him, so I went to him. No matter how low the water, how high and dry the logs, and how persuasive I was, Keno never set foot on the jam—not even in winter, when the logs were frozen in place and as stable as a dance floor.

"Here, come on, boy," I called. He wanted no part of our project. He wouldn't run away from me, but he wouldn't come, either. He lay with his nose on his paws and calmly watched me come to get him. Even when I was right beside him, calling his name, he wouldn't stand up, but finally he rolled over on his back in submission.

He was a load, but I carried him across the jam and stepped with him onto the raft where Jerry waited. I made him lie down. Jerry pushed us off. Keno was shivering, in spite of my telling him what a foolish thing he was for not enjoying this expense-paid luxury cruise.

"This is the 'S.S. *Davy Jones,*' " I whispered in his ear, "and she's bound across the seven seas for Samoa, Sumatra, Singapore, the Sudan, and . . . and . . ."

I'd started a string and needed another s-word. "And . . . the Stygian shore." I'd heard it in school.

But this time my silly words didn't work. The instant I loosened my grip around his neck to work the rope, Keno scrambled overboard in a grand belly flop like a bull elephant and swam for shore. When he climbed up the muddy bank, he shook himself three times in mighty muscle waves that rippled the fur from his nose to his tail. He rolled a few times in the tall grass behind the sheds, then trotted to the yard, head high, without a backward glance. We'd gone too far, and he was through with us.

"Some sailor he is," Jerry laughed. But I felt bad for making him come when he didn't want to.

Later, Dennis was on the raft, handling his own line while Jerry and I sat in the shade, under the brush, on a smooth, whitened log. Half buried in the mud, it had been there as long as I could remember. Jerry got busy with his pocketknife, cutting letters into the soft wood.

"What are you making?" I asked.

"You'll see," he said.

Watching somebody create something inch by inch like that is tiresome, so I soon went back to looking at Dennis, who never seemed to tire of gently poling up and down, up and down, in front of us. Watching him was tiresome, too.

"There. Look at that." Jerry's voice startled me. I'd been half dozing in the afternoon heat.

I looked at the crooked letters he'd dug into the white wood:

RAFT   AUG 57
JERRY   JAMIE

"Real good," I said.

"You want Denise's name on here?"

"Dennis? No. No, I don't think so."

"Good, 'cause he's not part of this. Sure, he helped us today, but he's not really part of this deal. This raft and this carving—they're for us, aren't they?"

"Sure."

"Somebody will find this wore-out old log years from now," Jerry said, "and know something about us— like what great sailors we were."

"Oh, yeah, right," I said. "That's what they'll know, all right."

Jerry perfected his carving while I stood up and skipped rocks across the calm water, coming close enough to Dennis a time or two for him to say, "Hey." But I wasn't going to hit him.

Jerry folded up his knife and stood to stretch. "Hey, Denise," he called. "You tired of that thing yet?"

"No." But he started pulling himself back in anyway.

Jerry turned to me, "I wonder what it would be like down at the sandbar. It's quiet water there, too."

I looked at him doubtfully. "I wondered about that. But there's nothing to tie to."

"We could hold the rope," Jerry said. "With three of us, it wouldn't be a problem."

"I guess not," I said. "I don't know."

"Just for the change," he said. "If it's not safe, we can come back here."

I thought about it. "Okay," I said.

We studied the situation. The sandbar was halfway down our south pasture. For the first hundred yards or so, the brush was too thick and overlapped the water too far for anyone on shore to be able to walk along holding the rope. Someone would have to ride downriver on his own. I felt nervous about that, especially after Dad had asked us to use the rope, but it was either that or pack the raft along the shore. Jerry volunteered for the ride.

Dennis and I ran ahead around the brush and watched Jerry come. He was poling carefully, staying close to shore, and he soon cleared the brush and came near enough to toss me the line. At that, he immediately pushed farther out until his pole no longer touched bottom. He sat down and let the current take him. By the time I felt the tug on the rope, he was below the lower end of the bar. He still had very little speed, but I was surprised at how much harder it was to hold him here than up at the logjam, where we had quiet water. With nothing to tie to, I had to dig my heels into the sand. And towing him back was like pulling a balky calf on a lasso.

We'd have to be careful here. The current was slow, but strong.

We each took our turns, but neither Dennis nor I went out nearly as far as Jerry did before sitting down to enjoy the ride. Twenty feet out was far enough for me. Even there, the pole barely reached bottom, which made me nervous. I was getting braver, though.

After a while, we pulled the raft up on the sand to rest. The sun wears a person out. I thought of the many times Dad and I had fished off the sandbar for suckers, using long bamboo poles. Deep, slow water was what suckers liked. Once, a few years back, I'd caught Dad in the cheek with my hook when I'd reared back to cast.

There was no shade, but we all lay on the sand. I scraped away the top layer of hot sand to lay facedown and put my cheek on my folded arms. I thought about running back to the storage house to get a watermelon and to tell Mom where we were, in case she hadn't seen us come down here, but I decided to rest a minute first. The four o'clock sun on my back was hot and relaxing.

I thought how this was the perfect day, the day the raft was launched at last, the day we'd waited for. And though I never would have expected Dennis Leeper to be part of it, even that didn't seem like such a problem right now.

The world needed more days like this.

seven

"One more spin?"

Jerry's voice sounded far away. I'd dozed again. Two naps in one afternoon! It must have been the heat, plus getting up early to hoe.

I opened my eyes and found myself face to face with a fish carcass—all backbone and ribs and fins and strips of withered black skin. It startled me instantly awake, and I jerked back. It was one of the many sucker skeletons that littered the sand, leftovers from my fishing success off the sandbar, but I wasn't used to seeing them at ground level. It wasn't there when I dozed off; Jerry must have moved it there to scare me.

I sat up to see Dennis towing Jerry back in from a ride. I threw the fish skeleton at Jerry. He laughed as it splashed near him.

"Anybody want to get on here with me?" he called. I was closest. "Good. With you on here for balance, I can pole harder," Jerry explained. "Let's get out as far as we can."

"Well, not too far, Captain," I said.

He ignored me. "Hold tight," he said to Dennis.

Jerry poled out until I said, "That's far enough,

Jerry. With two of us on here, let's not press our luck." He pulled in the pole and we sat back to enjoy the ride.

Dennis waited until we'd moved way past him and the rope was tightening in his hands before he started to jog through the loose sand. He wasn't yet making any effort to try and stop us, but was letting himself be sort of towed down the sandbar to give us more room to float.

"Oh, man, I hope . . . ," I started. I suddenly realized that none of us had tried to hold the rope with two people on the raft since moving to the sandbar. It would be heavy.

Then Dennis fell. With the sand pulling at his feet, he fell. It was a simple act. But in that single, irreversible instant, everything changed in the world.

It seemed to happen in slow motion. Dennis fell, and the rope flew from his hands like an escaping bird. He got up on his knees and straightened his glasses, a startled look on his face. Standing again quickly, he ran after the line, now slithering like a bull snake across the last stretch of sand. He dived for it too late.

"Denise!" Jerry shouted in unison with my "Dennis!" But our shouts only slowed him down as he obediently paused to look our way. He recovered and went after the rope that now skimmed across the surface of the water below the sandbar. Even the river didn't stop him, I'll say that for him, and he splashed in up to his knees.

He lunged, then straightened up in waist-deep water, pushing at his glasses with one hand and holding the end of the rope in the other.

"I got it!" he called triumphantly as he lifted the end of the rope for us to see.

"Watch out!" Jerry called. "Hold on! Both hands!"

I started, "He'll never be able . . ."

Had the slope been more gradual, the raft not weighted down by two people, the water shallower, or Dennis stronger, maybe he could have managed. But in water to the waist it's hard to maneuver, and we were way too heavy for him to hold. The instant he held up the line to show us he had it, he was yanked forward, like he'd lassoed a freight train.

This time, he'd locked on and wasn't about to let go. But there was no place for him to step. He was jerked off his feet and suddenly, no longer our anchor, he was in tow behind us like a fish on the end of a line, struggling and fighting the water.

"Oh, my gosh," I whispered. "I knew it. I knew it."

"Dennis!" Jerry called. "Try to . . ."

"Help me," he sputtered as he fought to keep his head up, the same words he'd used on the cliff Saturday.

"Swim," Jerry called. "Geez, can you swim, kid?"

There was no answer, but Dennis did start a sort of dog paddle and managed to keep his nose above water.

"Head for shore!" Jerry yelled. "Head for shore right now!" It was our only chance. But Dennis had his eyes fixed on the raft, his safety and hope. We'd have had to shoot him to change his focus. When it was clear he wasn't about to turn away and wasn't a good enough swimmer to make it to shore, anyway, Jerry gave up the idea and ordered, "Let's pull him in."

In a moment, we had Dennis aboard, and he lay gasping across the logs. There was room for three of us, but it was a little tight.

Jerry tried the pole but couldn't find the bottom, no matter how far down he reached. I didn't want to see that.

My mouth was dry, like it was when the fire got away from me on Friday. I tried to calm my pounding heart and make myself think. I had to think. How could we get out of here? Who could help us?

Already, we were too far from the house to be heard if we yelled, and it didn't seem right to shout at the sky and the trees and the hills, like madhouse escapees, with no one around to hear. A driver on the road might see us, but there were no cars in sight.

"Maybe I could tow us in," Jerry said. But we knew it wouldn't work. Even for a good swimmer like Jerry, we were too far out by now, and towing the raft would be like towing a barge. Maybe Jerry could have made it to shore on his own, but I didn't think he would go and leave the two of us out here to end up who knows where.

We sailed on our quiet, desperate way, and there seemed nothing we could do about it.

Nobody spoke for a while. Suddenly, Jerry broke the stillness. "Hey, this is great, you know!" he exclaimed.

Clearly, he'd lost his mind.

"Hey, think about it! This is the adventure we wanted, isn't it? A raft is to sail on, isn't it?"

I didn't know who he was trying to convince. Maybe it was another form of his confident adult talk.

He went on. "No problem. We'll just sail along here until we drift over far enough that we can pole out, or something."

Oh, right. No problem.

"The dams. What about the dams?" Dennis said. He was sitting up now, his lips blue. His question shut up Jerry's nonsense adventure talk. "Never make it over the dams," Dennis said.

I'd hiked down the river and seen the dams up close—two of them, spaced close to a mile apart.

"Never make it over the dams," Dennis said again, his voice weak and quivery.

"Oh, cripes. Would you shut up, for crying out loud!" Jerry snapped. It seemed he'd quickly given up the idea of a pleasant sailing adventure.

From then on, Dennis sat motionless and kind of slumped over in the middle of the raft, and he didn't say any more.

We were moving past the flume now, high on the hill. It felt like Saturday's flume walk was ages past. Even today's breakfast was part of a lost world.

The mill whistle sounded, weak and distant—on the wrong side of the river as it echoed back off the hill.

The five o'clock whistle. Dad's hand on the cord, signaling the mill workers to close down. I wished we could signal *him*. In a few minutes, he would get in his pickup and head home. But it would take him twenty minutes or more to get through town and up to this point on our road, even if he didn't stop for anything in town. By then, it would be too late. We were already starting into the curve behind the Big Ranch field, and the river wouldn't come back in sight of the road again until down below the second dam. In another few minutes, nobody would be able to see us at all.

We constantly checked the road for signs of a car. Even Arlie Leeper's old truck would be a welcome sight right now.

We were farther from shore now and close to the middle of the wide river. If not for what lay ahead, it would have been a pleasant ride, as smooth as a baby carriage.

Soon I sensed us slowing down. "We're into the backup of the dam, I think," I said.

Jerry lay down and tried the pole again. A few times earlier, he had scraped bottom with it, but never enough to get any leverage. Now his longest reach, clear to the armpit, touched nothing at all.

For a few minutes we lay down and tried paddling in unison with our hands and arms toward shore, but we could see no progress. The river had narrowed some and neither shore was that far, but we had no way to reach either one. We gave up the effort and just waited. Choice was gone for us. We went where the river chose to take us.

"Okay, let's think now," Jerry said. "Let's think hard what we can do. We're going over the dam. There's nothing we can do about that. We are going over." He was right. Even a driver stopping on the road right now couldn't reach us in time, unless he was towing a speedboat. That was about as likely as a driver hauling a Navy diving team or a helicopter on a flatbed truck. "So since we're going over, we have to figure out how we can stay on this thing when we do."

Dennis was mute, staring downstream as if in a trance. I was thinking, but I had no answer, either.

Since Jerry'd never seen the dams up close, he had me tell him about them.

I tried to remember how each one was built. They were both fully under water. Their job was to slow down and back up the river. The second one fed the canal that ran across the valley. The first one had no clear purpose; maybe it was an early, failed attempt at a canal project, I didn't know. No part of either structure was visible, except for a number of thin posts that projected straight up from the first one. The water rolled over that dam in a fairly gentle four- or five-foot slope, and it looked like you might be able to go over it in a big inner tube if you held on tight. Although as scared as I was of the water, I personally would never have tried it on purpose.

The second dam had a longer and steeper drop. The water fell over that one like a waterfall and churned up a frothy turbulence at the base. No raft would stay upright at the bottom of the second dam, I was sure of that.

I'd just finished describing the dams when Jerry

pointed downstream and said, "The posts." The row of metal pipes, apparently left over from the dam's construction, was visible now, protruding from the water like matchsticks. There were six of them across the river, spaced evenly except for gaps where two were missing, and they stuck up four or five feet out of the water.

Could we somehow hold on or tie up to one of them? It was a desperate idea. And it wasn't likely, with the force the water would exert on us at that point. Even if all three of us somehow could manage to hold on to a post, how would it help? Nothing short of that fictional helicopter could rescue us from a perch smack on the brim of a waterfall.

"I can hear it," Jerry said. I could barely make it out—the distant, muffled sound of water, tons and tons of water, dropping heavily over the precipice.

I'd kept myself pretty calm for the last few minutes, but the deep, penetrating rumble of that water about did me in.

"We'd better lay down," I said. My voice sounded thin and weak. "We can hold on better."

"Yeah, okay," Jerry agreed. When Dennis didn't move, Jerry put a hand on his arm and said, "Lay down and hold on. Come on, now. Like this." It was almost gentle.

Dennis moved into position between us. After trying, without success, for the bottom once more, Jerry pulled in the pole and put it beside him. I gripped the edge of the raft above my head with one hand. With the other, I reached down and found a good place to grip the bottom structure, although the river was too cold to leave my hand in until the time came. I stared down into the black-green water and tried not to think.

We were far enough from shore that, from this viewpoint, it felt like we were sitting still in the middle of a smooth lake. Only the increasing sound and the posts slowly growing taller gave evidence of movement.

We were fully out of sight of the road now, into the curve of the river. Looking back upstream, my eye caught the hawk I'd seen often this summer, a tiny speck as he winged up over the big hill and into the valley for his afternoon flight. He was climbing high up over the south pasture, today's hunting ground, starting his slow and watchful circle.

The features of neither bank were familiar to me here, and I felt myself slowly sliding out of the world I knew. It was more dreamy and unreal than scary. I thought of Mom back at the house. I could look back and see, from where the fire's black smudge met the green ribbon of the ditch, where our house had to be. But I couldn't see it—not even the roof—nothing except the very tops of the walnut trees.

The rumble was increasing. We said little now—Jerry and I—and Dennis hadn't spoken since he was told to shut up. He lay quietly and looked down into the water, seemingly calm, but his breathing gave him away. It was rapid and shallow, like a small animal's. Hearing it made me concentrate on keeping my own breathing as near its normal rhythm as possible.

Downstream, we could see now where the flat expanse of the river disappeared over the dam. It reminded me of drawings I'd seen in books of what the ancient sailors thought the farthest reaches of the flat earth would be like—where the sea dropped off the edge of the world. "Past this point, there be dragons," they wrote along the edges of their old maps. It looked like we were about to find out.

I looked upstream one last time, just at the moment the hawk folded his wings tight and dropped like a spear over the south pasture, heading for the ground at a hundred miles an hour. Before he went out of sight behind the riverside brush he seemed to slow down, and even though he was too far away for me to tell, I knew his razor-like talons would be opening and sliding forward for the attack. It was a dive that meant sure death for whatever small creature he'd spotted.

"Feet first," Jerry said. Using our hands to paddle, we managed to keep ourselves pointed more or less backward.

The noise of the falls was growing rapidly now, and when I turned and looked again, the posts were much taller. I found my handhold in the cold water. Clammy sweat dripped from under my arms.

"Oh, crap. We're going to hit a post," Jerry called over the din. We were headed straight for one of the metal pipes, and over my shoulder I watched it grow.

Suddenly, we crested the edge of the dam and the rushing noise increased manyfold into a booming thunder that shook my stomach. We all involuntarily jerked our heads around to look.

We'd entered the first gentle curve of the downturning water like a roller coaster at the fair barely starting its plunge, when we struck the post at a spot right between Dennis's feet. It couldn't have been a better midship hit if we'd aimed for it.

Hitting the pipe stopped us with a shudder and cold water lapped up on our chests, taking away our breath as the river tried to run over us. Slowly, so slowly, we started our inevitable pivot around this last obstacle. We wouldn't be going over feet first after all, but sideways, with Jerry on the bottom and me on the top, and nothing could be done about it now.

In the water, a few feet under our faces, I saw the gray cement of the dam—partly smooth, partly a jumble of broken blocks—interspersed with a network of metal reinforcing rods.

I put my head down, held what breath I could get, and tightened my grip as we started our slide off the edge of the world.

eight

We tipped and fell. We hit on an edge and sliced sideways into the shockingly cold water. But we quickly bounced up. I opened my eyes as we sped rapidly away.

Letting myself breathe again, I wanted to shout for joy. We were still on the raft, wet but still upright! We'd survived the first dam!

I loosened my grip somewhat, lessening the pain in my knuckles.

A second later we stopped, suddenly, spinning halfway around and with a tremendous jolt, like a car hitting a cement wall. I rolled into Dennis. He rolled, too, and I grabbed him.

I looked up. Jerry was gone!

In an instant, the pole Jerry had been lying on rose up out of the water like a javelin, fell over, and headed downstream. Jerry bobbed up next, facing us and looking tremendously startled. He made several strokes in our direction, but he was already a few yards downstream and the river was carrying him rapidly away. For some reason, we weren't moving, and he stood no chance of fighting his way back against the wild current. He soon gave up and struck out downstream.

We could only hold on and watch him go. He turned around once when he was out of the white water and shouted, but no voice could penetrate the din behind us. He made some hand signals that I couldn't understand, then turned and swam away, angling toward the west bank.

I turned my attention to our situation. What had stopped us? We must have hit something. But I soon saw the truth. It was simple—our rope was caught on the dam.

Long forgotten after we pulled Dennis in, the line had trailed in the water as we went over, and a knot must have caught on the underwater metalwork of the dam. The sudden stop had rolled Jerry off. And we were now tied to the dam, fifteen to twenty feet below it, toward the tail end of its rough wake.

"Dennis, move over!" I shouted. But he couldn't hear me. I had to gesture and pull on his arm to get him to understand. Adjusting our positions to make up for Jerry's absence leveled us out, but the raft still pitched wildly. Unable to move freely with the river, it jumped at the end of its rope like a wild colt lassoed for the first time. Water swirled up around us, especially on our legs.

I kept my eye on Jerry for as long as I could see him. From our low angle on the water, I lost sight of him before I saw if he actually reached the brush on the far bank. I knew I would certainly have drowned had it been me, and from what I'd seen of Dennis's dog paddle, he wouldn't have made it, either. But Jerry was taking long, smooth strokes when I last saw him and, knowing his swimming ability, I was sure he would make it.

I focused again on our situation. Dennis and I were completely soaked, and even in the late afternoon sun, soon very cold. It might have been better to sit up, but the ride was so rough I feared we'd be pitched in. It took a lot of effort just to hold on.

Once, when I looked at Dennis, he was crying with his face on his arms. I didn't like it and told him to stop, but he couldn't hear me. I had to poke him until he raised his head and looked at me. His face was all crinkled up, and when he lay back down, I couldn't tell if he had stopped or not.

At first I cursed the rope that had stopped us and thrown Jerry off, but the more I thought about it, the more I realized it was our salvation, at least temporarily. Since it seemed certain we couldn't survive the second dam, the rope gave us a chance. If it held, and if Jerry made it to shore, and if we could hold on long enough, someone could put in a boat and come to us. Maybe we hadn't fallen off the edge of the world, after all.

The framework underneath the raft might not stand the pressure the rope was putting on it, so I spent a lot of time gripping the line in my hands in case the wood tore loose. But it was a strain on my arms, and I often needed to rest.

By gesturing and pointing, I got Dennis to hold the

rope once, but he paid no attention to what he was doing. If it had torn loose, he wouldn't have been prepared, so I took it back from him.

I watched the west bank, even though I knew it was still too soon for help to appear. After he made it out of the water, Jerry would have to walk—or run if he felt up to it—a good half mile to the nearest house on the upper edge of town, the Carltons'. I wasn't sure they had a phone. If no one was home there, he'd have to go on another quarter mile to the Sheasbys'. I was pretty certain they didn't have a phone.

Somebody would have to drive Jerry into town for help—probably to his folks' store, where, if the timing was lucky, Dad might have stopped. They'd need to locate a motorized fishing boat. There were only two or three of those in the whole valley that I knew of, so that could take a while. Then they'd have to tow it up an old road by the railroad tracks and get it in the water.

I tried to keep track of the time and think through how long it would take for all this to happen. It felt like it had been a long time, but it was hard to tell, since it was hard to think about anything except the cold and holding on. Dennis was shivering steadily now.

"On your hands and knees, Dennis," I shouted. I showed him the way I'd discovered to get mostly up out of the water. It was warmer, but it was harder to hold on, the way the raft was bouncing around. Our arms tired quickly and we had to lie back down often to relax our grip.

It was odd that my fear was less at the moment. Just being around deep water usually spooked me, but the terror I'd felt going over the dam must have used up about all the fright in me at the moment. Or maybe the cold water had deadened me, because other than being naturally careful about not falling off, I wasn't much worried about riding these waves now that rescue looked possible. The thought of tearing loose to go on downstream did concern me, though, so I held the rope as much as I could.

Time went by and the sun finally dropped behind the west hill. Though it wouldn't be down yet at our house or at most other places in the valley, a knoll between the highway and the river shaded this spot. Instantly I felt colder, and I wondered what would happen if we were still out here when darkness came. I was sure we couldn't hold on through a whole night. We were both shivering now, Dennis almost violently.

I thought about Jerry. Maybe instead of coming out down by Carlton's, he would climb from the river far enough above town to hike up across Ashcroft's field, which sloped off the south side of the hill that now blocked the sun. In that case, he'd head straight up to the highway and hitch a ride to the store. How long would that take, and how long had it been? A half hour? An hour? I couldn't tell, but it gave me something to think about.

Then it happened. During one of my frequent pauses to rest my arms, we tore free with a lurch, leaving behind a piece of our wooden frame dancing in the waves at the end of the line. I grabbed for the rope, but it was too late.

"Oh, no!" My fear came back with the speed of lightning and found lodging in the pit of my stomach.

But in the short run, things were improved. No longer tied to the dam's wild wake, the raft immediately popped up again out of the cold water. And away from the dam, the stream was slow and smooth, so we could sit up. As the noise of the falls receded, it was like a pressing weight was being lifted from the top of my head. I could now hear again—including the sound of Dennis's teeth clacking together.

I hoped Jerry had made it—certainly for his sake, but also for ours. But as yet there was no sign of anyone on the river road to the west. They'd have to hurry. I wasn't sure anyone could drive up, launch a boat, and get clear out to us before we'd reach the second dam. I figured we had maybe twenty minutes to be saved.

We'd been floating placidly for a few minutes, and I was concentrating on the west bank when Dennis startled me by coming out of his trance long enough to raise his arm and point behind us without a word. I turned and saw a startling sight: five of our cans trailing out of reach behind us, like lemmings marching in a straight line to the sea.

"No!" I said. Not only my hands and feet but my brain must have been numbed for me not to realize the cans would escape when the rope ripped a gap in the frame, nor to notice how we had tilted and dropped lower in the water.

Immediately, I lay down and put my arm across the opening to keep from losing more of the cans, alternating arms often because of the cold water. My position caused us to tip more, and I had to tell Dennis to move farther the other way to balance us.

"What's that?" I asked. It sounded like a distant motor. The direction was hard to pinpoint, but it was a vehicle, perhaps a truck of some kind. Scanning the access road to the west, I saw nothing. It had to be on the dirt road to my house, now hidden from our view.

"Maybe if we stand, they can see us. Let's try it, Dennis. Hurry." I doubted our chances, since we were now invisible across the Big Ranch field, but we had to try.

Dennis tried to stand, but he was so shaky and shivery he couldn't do it. I had him face me. Holding hands like dancers and standing up together we made it; but we still couldn't see the road. I got him to shout with me in unison. "Hello-o-o-o-o. Hello-o-o-o-o. He-l-l-lp! He-l-l-lp!" It was no use. In a few seconds the sound faded, and our hopes with it. Whatever vehicle it was, it was gone without our even seeing its dust.

We sat back down. "Worth a try." That's what I said, but I wasn't sure, because while we stood, two more cans had come out. One of them was only a few feet behind us, and by paddling hard upstream with our hands, we were able to slow ourselves down enough for me to grab it. Pressing down against its surprising buoyancy, I pushed it back under us with a vicious thrust, like it was a wayward animal I wanted to discipline. It felt like a victory, but I wasn't sure it would matter much in the long run.

"They'll have to hurry," I said, mostly to myself. "Half our cans are gone. They'll just have to hurry." I took up my reclining position again to hold in the remaining cans.

Standing and shouting had made me feel a little warmer, but Dennis was shaking as hard as ever.

I lay down and tried to think what to do when we went over the second dam, but I couldn't think of anything. We must be about halfway there by now. I'd hoped we would catch up with the sun so we could warm up a little, but the shadow of the west hill crept ahead of us down the river.

The river had widened some, but we had drifted a little off center and the eastern bank was only a few dozen yards away. I tried paddling hard with my hands for a few minutes to see if we could reach the bank, but we didn't move perceptibly. Without a pole or some way to paddle, it was hopeless—maddeningly hopeless.

It was so quiet I could hear the buzzing and crackling of the locusts on the near bank, so it surprised me when Dennis spoke.

"Thank you," he said softly. He sat rigidly on a corner, staring out across the river. He wasn't looking at me.

"What?" I asked, and raised my head.

"For letting me on your raft."

It was an odd thing to be thankful for right now.

"Most people don't let me do things with them," he said.

I had nothing to say. I didn't deserve any thanks. It's true I was never a ringleader, but lots and lots of times I'd enjoyed the spectacle of Leeper-suffering as much as anybody. I had gone along, and I knew my silence didn't justify me. I was only quieter than some, not better.

Dennis looked at me straight on for a moment and nodded his head as if satisfied. I put my face back down on my forearm.

After a minute, I looked up. "We're going to be okay, you know," I said. "We are." But Dennis was again looking vacantly out across the water and gave no sign that he heard me.

We were slowing down some, and I was becoming gradually aware of a dull grumble. I raised up and looked downstream. Even at this distance, the sound seemed deeper and more threatening than on the first dam, and I thought of the steep drop we would face. I lay back down and tried somehow to loosen the tightening knot in my gut. Where were they?

Finally, in one of my regular scans of the west shore, I saw a movement—a car over by the tracks, a blue one like the Ford Uncle Oscar, Jerry's dad, drove.

"There they are!" I shouted as I stood up carefully and started waving. Jerry had made it, after all!

But where was the boat? The blue car had now

turned around and was heading back downstream. What was going on?

"Didn't they bring a boat, for crying out loud?" I exclaimed.

Farther down the brushy shoreline I saw a pickup, with Jerry standing right on top of the cab, pointing downstream and waving so hard I thought he would fall off. I signaled back with both arms and shouted—like they didn't already know we were here. Other cars were arriving, and I could make out an empty boat trailer behind the pickup. But where was the boat?

I turned to see that while I was waving, we'd lost the can we'd retrieved. I dropped down and felt underneath once more; no other cans were close to the opening at the moment.

At once, it was terrifyingly clear. Uncle Oscar—or whoever was in the blue car—had been coming upstream for a look, but the other vehicles were all *below* the second dam. The boat must already be in the water down there!

"I guess they couldn't get a boat in up here, or didn't have time to, when they saw we'd broken loose." I spoke loudly over the increasing rumble. "We'll have to go over before they can get to us." It was a horrible thought. "Oh, Lord, please," I breathed.

Dennis showed no interest in any of these things. He looked, but he didn't say anything. He seemed without hope.

I stood again, balancing myself with a hand on

Dennis's shoulder, and looked downstream. "There!" I pointed. "There they are." Twenty yards below the dam, in the middle of the river and right at the edge of the sunlight, was the boat. I could just see it over the lip of the dam. The boat was aimed upstream, as close to the spray and wild water as it could get without fighting the bucking wake too much. Three men sat waiting in the little wooden vessel, running the outboard at the right speed to hold it in place. It was all they could do for now. Without wings, they couldn't come to us; we'd have to go to them.

They all three simultaneously pointed at us as we came into view, and the man handling the motor moved the tiller sharply to line them up right below where we would come over. Another man gestured and appeared to be giving directions to the motor man, while the third waved frantically at us.

Now we would be saved. Oh, God, help us be saved.

My certainty that all would be well didn't take away my great fear—increasing with each foot we gained—of falling over this dam. If these falls were as steep as I remembered, I was absolutely certain we would capsize at the bottom. Somehow, we would have to keep ourselves afloat in that wild water long enough to be picked up.

I'd given up worrying about the cans floating out; that didn't matter now. But seeing one more pop out gave me an idea.

"Dennis!" I called. "Here! Hold a can!" Frantically,

I knelt and reached under the raft, but none was near the opening now. How was it they could come out so easily when we wanted them to stay put, but fail us when we needed them?

The noise was increasing greatly. We were running out of time. Just then my fingers reached the rim of a can. I yanked it out.

"Here," I yelled over the noise. "Lay down, and hold this in your arms." I pushed the can to Dennis and searched wildly for another. I found one and jerked it free a few seconds before we breached the edge of the dam and the full force of the noise came to my ears— a deep, pounding throb, stunning in its intensity. I lay down. I grabbed Dennis by the wrist for a moment, then involuntarily let go to clutch the can to my chest as I looked down into the maelstrom and we started to tip.

"Hold tight, Dennis!" I screamed. "Hold on tight!" I was sure he couldn't hear me. He was already dropping over the edge.

Sideways, we pitched over in free fall, toppling into the churning water, the raft smashing down on top of us. The roar in my ears changed to pain, a deafening pulsing, like it might feel to be inside a thunderstorm. My eyes came open, but I could see only white, as billions of tiny bubbles were whipped into a boiling froth.

The next few awful moments were a confusion of thrashing and tumbling and fighting the water, of trying to tell up from down. Of bobbing to the surface at least twice for a panicky gasp of breath. Of seeing the men in the boat struggling to reach us, yet still being so far away. Of losing my can, gaining another, and losing it too in the tearing water. Of a burning in my nose, of choking, of swallowing water and more water. Of a slow descent into darkness. And finally, of a surprising loss of fear, replaced at last by a vague, textureless sorrow.

An odd buzzing grew in my ears as the light was going away. It was like going under the ether when I was eight and had my tonsils out. Gradually, there came a welcome, peaceful stillness.

My last conscious thoughts were clear: first, the memory of telling Dennis we would be okay, and now knowing it might not be, probably wouldn't be. And second, the recognition that one of the men in the boat—the one waving with welcoming arms—was my own dad. The man so afraid of water that he'd never before been in a boat in his life had come to save me.

nine

I lay in my bed unmoving—not certain, for a time, that I was really awake. The line between sleep and wakefulness was thin this morning, and I had drifted across it at some point but couldn't remember just when.

My body felt drugged, as if I had no power to move a single limb. Even opening my eyelids was an effort. When I finally did force myself to do that, my room looked different and new and strange, even though I'd awakened in it every morning for years.

The square glass light cover, with its scalloped edges and sweeping floral design, stared down at me from the ceiling. In the corner, hanging on its bent rod, was the striped curtain Mom had sewn for my wooden wardrobe.

On top of the wardrobe sat my large, unfinished balsa model of a B-29 bomber, a dusty shell that I'd set aside last winter when I'd tired, finally and permanently, of the weeks of tedious cutting and gluing of the soft wood. I knew I would never finish the ribbed fuselage to the point of cementing on the silver paper skin. But I hadn't been able to throw it out; I'd put too much work into it.

I closed my eyes and remembered other things: My father's frightened face in the boat last night as we went over the dam toward him. Being tossed around under the heavy water. Bobbing up and going under again. The terror of choking. The slow fade into blackness.

These unbidden memories all appeared again and again in my mind, like a pack of mangy stray cats that showed up at our place one spring and wouldn't be driven away.

I remembered coming to, in the boat, in my father's arms, my head on his lap. His face was white as he called my name and rubbed my cheeks, gripping my hand like he'd never let go. I couldn't speak. I had to turn and vomit river water over the side.

I lay for a long time on my back in the bottom of the boat, weak, looking up at the sky—the surprising, wonderful sky that had never been so blue and so bright. Eventually, I noticed my ear was bleeding a little—probably from when the raft fell down on top of us.

As the motor raced, we were in sunlight, in shade, back in sunlight. It seemed odd, but I didn't have the energy to think about why it was happening. I didn't care about anything except being alive. But after a time, as I started to feel better, I asked why we weren't at the shore yet. We'd been moving for such a long time.

One of the men said, "We're looking for the Leeper boy, son." I looked around. For the first time, I realized, with horror, that Dennis wasn't with us.

Shame washed over me like a wave. I hadn't even noticed.

I looked at Dad's ashen face as he searched the water. I wanted to help, but I had no strength and I was starting to shiver. Finally, I lay back again and tried not to think. Just let this day, once and for all, finally and forever, come to an end.

The boat was making repeated circuits up and down for hundreds of yards, from the shade into the sunlight, looking, looking, looking for Dennis, until the growing shadow of the west hills crept down the river and the light was gone.

As dusk finally overtook us, one of the men said, "We did all we could," and the boat turned sharply toward the west bank.

I raised up on an elbow and looked. A small group of people waited on the shore now as more cars had arrived. Someone had their headlights on, like two beacons in the growing darkness.

At the bank, I tried to get out of the boat and was surprised to find I needed my dad's arm around me to stand. There was little talk, but every eye was on me as we made our slow way to the car.

Jerry was there, shivering a little and still wet. "Jamie," he said, and put his hand on my shoulder and touched my bleeding ear with his finger. "Jamie. From here, we couldn't tell. We couldn't tell who it was they pulled in."

Jack G., the deputy, was just getting there and took

charge of things right away. He asked me a few questions as I sat in the car, how it happened, and what the blazes we thought we were doing on the river anyway. For as gruff as he was, I was surprised when he said, "You did a good job, Slim," before telling us we could go. He went to talk to Jerry as we drove away.

I wondered if Arlie Leeper was there, but I didn't see him.

Not much was said on the drive back to the store. Uncle Oscar drove us, with Dad and me in the back seat.

It was near dark by the time we got there. There was a small crowd outside the store, mostly women. They all stared at me in silence or with murmuring words. We went in for a moment. Aunt Lois came out from behind the counter, hugged me tight against her in my wet clothes, tears running down her face, and then got a blanket to wrap around my shoulders. Dad asked her to call Mom, then we climbed into the pickup and headed for home.

The ride seemed to take a long time. Dad turned on the heater for me with the windows up. The blower smelled of dust. By the time we pulled in under the locust tree, he was wiping sweat from his face, but I still wasn't warm.

The rest was a jumble of still-frame images: Mom waiting out front and running to me before I even got out of the truck, with tears and crushing hugs and frantic kisses. Marie holding me around the waist and not letting go as I walked across the yard. Keno licking my hand. In the house, Mom putting stinging antiseptic on my ear. Getting out of my wet clothes and drying off. Falling into bed. Dad kissing my cheek, his whiskers rough, his face still stricken. The three of them standing for a long time, looking at me in the light from the kitchen like I was a lost treasure now returned. Finally starting to feel warm with a hot-water bottle and extra covers. And tiredness—exquisite, numbing tiredness.

My brain wasn't working very well, but it didn't seem real that I was in my warm bed and Dennis was still somewhere in the cold river. I tried to make myself not think about it.

Finally, sleep. Kind sleep. I wanted it to last forever.

But now it was morning—late morning likely, from the color of the light and the heat in the air. The only sound in the house was of water running through the pipes under the house—the sprinkler. A half mile up the road at Palmer's, a dog barked sporadically in a cheerless and lackadaisical way.

I still didn't feel like I could budge, but it was time to try. I moved my head and saw a trace of blood on my pillow. My ear was tender.

My legs moved like logs when, one at a time, I placed my feet on the cool linoleum. After sitting for a few minutes, I managed to stand up and dress. I was slow at it, but by the time I was done I felt more like I was alive again.

I went to the kitchen for a drink. My lips were

cracked and sunburned, and even after two glasses of cold water my mouth still tasted like spoiled milk. The old electric alarm clock on the counter—banished from Mom's bedroom because of its whirring and grinding noises—read 10:36.

No one was in the house, but the pressure cooker hissed on the stove and the gauge read 250, right where Mom liked it, ten degrees below the red zone. Glancing at the gauge was an automatic response. I'd heard enough times of how old Mrs. Beckstrand let hers get too hot and then tried to open it. The lid broke her wrist before putting a hole in the ceiling and lodging in the attic. Years ago, before I understood the danger, I had once opened a smaller pressure cooker to see what was for dinner. The lid landed on the floor, and the beets inside stained the ceiling with red polka dots before they hurtled down on me like volcanic cinders.

I saw no one on my way to the outhouse, nor on my way back, but it was so bright outside it hurt my eyes. I looked at the river without interest. It looked different to me somehow.

Back at the house I looked in each room, then opened the front door. There they were—Dad, Mom, and Marie—all seated on the torn old davenport we kept on the porch and snapping green beans into pans. Their hands stopped moving.

"What are you doing home?" I asked Dad, my voice still thick with sleep.

I couldn't figure it out; he never missed work—not

for sickness, farm chores, or anything else. "And why are you all out here?" It was cooler inside this time of day.

"To let you sleep," Mom answered. "How do you feel?"

"Okay, I guess. Tired." They all looked at me like I'd come from another world.

"Dad stayed home to help look for Dennis," Mom said.

"But they already found him," Marie said.

"They did?"

"Yes," Mom said. "Uncle Oscar called early."

Dad took it up from there, looking out across the field as he talked. "At daylight, in the shallows down by the bridge. It was a miracle to find him so soon. Washed up on some brush."

He said it even and steady, like a radio announcer telling the weather report. But when he finished, he looked down and made a sigh, cracked in the middle like it caught in his throat, then went back to the beans in his hands.

Several pans partly filled with broken pods sat on the floor and there was still a half bushel left to snap. The jars in the pressure cooker were probably filled with beans, too, I realized. Somebody had been up very early to pick so many.

Mom shook her head. "It's so sad," she said. She stood up and hugged me. I felt one of her quick, hot tears drop on my shirt. Over her shoulder, out in the sunlight, the sprinkler threw a circle of glinting diamonds onto grass that looked more brilliant and green than I'd ever seen it. Keno lay in his regular spot in the shade.

Mom checked my ear, then started into the house.

"The cooker's okay," I said. "I checked it."

"You'll want some breakfast," she said.

"No, I'm not hungry. Really. I'm not."

She sat down again, and nobody said any more for a time. I still didn't know why Dad was home once Dennis had been found, but I guessed it was to be with me.

I leaned on the porch railing and started on a handful of beans. Some of them gave sharp pops as we broke them into bite-size segments. With four of us at it, it sounded like a packet of tiny lady-finger firecrackers going off. Bean snapping was hard on the fingers after a while, and my hands were stiff today.

"Jamie," Mom said. The snapping stopped again.

"What?"

"I need to be sure you understand something. Your dad keeps feeling like this was his fault because he didn't stop you from making the raft. I've been telling him not to think that way."

I looked at Dad and shook my head. "No. That's not right. We'd have built that raft no matter what."

His face had some of that same desolate look he'd had last night in the boat. "I wish I'd kept you boys off that thing," he said quietly.

There was a pause, then Mom said, "Jamie, you may be blaming yourself somewhat, too, so I'm going to say something to both of you. It's a terrible, sad thing that happened. It will affect all of us for the rest of our days. But it's happened. And a person can spend every minute from here through eternity thinking about it and wishing things were different, and it doesn't change a thing."

Dad nodded, but his face was flat and sober.

Mom went on, her voice fierce and somewhat too loud, her finger raised. "You have to let it go, Dale—all of us do. We'll sorrow and we'll mourn, then we'll get past it. That's it. That's all we can do."

It was quiet for a long time, until Marie snapped another pod and a purple-green bean hit the edge of a pan with a soft ping and danced a wild jig across the floorboards to rest in a corner of the porch.

I knew Mom was right. At the moment, it didn't really make me feel any better, but still she was right.

One by one, we went back to work. Mom moved Marie to the floor so I could sit on the davenport.

After a time, I asked, "Did anybody tell Arlie? About finding Dennis?" The Leepers didn't have a phone.

"I saw Jack G. go by about a half hour after Uncle Oscar called," Mom said, waving her arm toward the road, "then come back down—oh, forty-five minutes later."

When the beans were done, we carried the pots in. By then, I was tired and ready to rest again, so I sat at the table with Marie. I noticed she was staying close to me. Nobody talked much as Mom and Dad washed beans and filled jars at the counter.

After lunch, I wanted a nap, so I dozed off to the sound of soft pinging from the kitchen, like BB's hitting faraway tin cans, as the lids sealed on a batch of cooling beans. Mom loved that sound of successful sealing and always counted each one out loud. She'd hear a ping and say "four" or "six" or whatever it happened to be. She could be in the middle of a conversation or in another room—even on the phone—but she'd still know right where she was in her count. She wasn't at peace until all seven jars from a canner load made their sealing known.

The nap left me feeling hot and groggy. Soon I remembered the newspaper and asked Dad if he'd picked it up yesterday. On Mondays, he always stopped at the store to buy the Sunday newspaper brought in from Boise a day late. It had a big colored comics section that I loved to read, usually sprawled on the davenport with the paper on the floor. It was a ritual with me.

He said yes, he'd bought it, and had been getting back in the truck when old Mr. Carlton and Jerry roared up honking and skidding in the gravel in front of the store, stopping about a foot from the front display window. Mr. Carlton was too old to drive, but he was the only one in Union who didn't know it.

"Must be still in the pickup." He stood to go out.

"I can get it, Dad." I went out and found the paper on the floorboards. It had water stains on the front page where I'd dripped river water on it. On the way back in, I stopped and looked at Dennis's old bike, abandoned under our tree where he'd left it. That was only yesterday morning, but it seemed a thousand years ago. It still wasn't real to me that he wouldn't ever be back to ride it home.

I was half dozing on the davenport when the phone rang—four shorts, our ring. It had rung quite a lot that day, as relatives and others called my folks to check on me. Jerry had called and talked to me a few minutes, too.

Mom answered it. She stood looking out the window and mostly listening. I knew it was Aunt Lois, and that she was telling a detailed story of some kind, and I could soon tell it was about Arlie.

I tried to figure it out from Mom's comments: "Oh? . . . Oh, my . . . The poor man . . . He didn't? But now he will? . . . Oh, good."

Dad came in from the kitchen and sat and listened. When Mom hung up, we looked at her expectantly. She patted her cheeks with both hands while she sat down.

"Lois says Arlie didn't want a funeral, at first. I guess when the deputy went up to tell him about finding his boy, Arlie wanted to come to town right then and get him and bury him himself up on his place." She shook her head.

"Jack G. told him he didn't think that was right or legal, and Arlie finally gave in and agreed to a burial in the cemetery. It took quite a bit more talking to get Arlie to see that a funeral would be the right thing."

"Why wouldn't he want a funeral?" I asked. "Because he doesn't like people?"

"Maybe, or he thinks people don't like him," Mom said. "No need for a funeral if you think nobody will come."

Arlie was right about that; the Leepers had no friends that I knew of. But it was sad that he hadn't wanted a funeral—sad for Dennis. I'd never heard of such a thing. Arlie would drop his boy in a hole in the ground out behind his barn or somewhere, and nobody would know Dennis had ever lived.

"Anyway, he finally agreed," Mom said, "And the funeral is Thursday at two. How sad it will be."

The rest of the afternoon I spent reading the newspaper and resting, not feeling up to much. Marie seemed to stay near me all day. Dad had told me earlier to rest as much as I wanted and not to worry about the chores, but I felt like I should help, and at chore time I went out and started to feed the chickens. Dad came out the back door, looked my way, and headed for the barn. I didn't mind getting out of milking. My arms and hands were sore.

There was a gray sky all afternoon. Supper was early, since Dad was home. During the meal, Mom started talking about last night. She'd called us to chores and when we didn't come, she had sent Marie to find us.

"She came back and scared me to death by saying you were nowhere to be seen, and neither was the raft. Just then, the phone rang. It was Lois saying that Jerry had come into the store, dripping wet, with the story."

It chilled me to hear Mom tell it, although she wasn't putting any dramatics into it at all.

"We prayed," Marie added. "We kneeled down by your bed, Jamie."

"Yes, we did," Mom said. "Then I milked and did the chores. There wasn't anything I could do, since all the men were already out looking for you, so I did the chores. I left Marie in the house to get the phone in case there was word. And we just waited and waited and waited." She looked away and her voice trailed off.

It made me hurt inside to think of what we put her through.

After supper, I heard Keno whining out back. He soon came up onto the porch and huddled against the house, like it was winter. I went out to talk to him and he stopped whining, but he wouldn't snap out of it. He sat with a wild look in his eyes as if he didn't know me, the hair on the back of his neck bristling up like a wild animal.

The other animals were acting strange, too. I'd never seen her do it before, but the cow stood in the field with her hooves planted wide apart and her head low, bellowing like somebody'd stolen a calf from her.

Several blackbirds flew in tight circles around the river trees, like they were caught in a giant churn, never lighting for more than a second and not making a sound. Even the chickens were restless and a few of them hopped around the yard in short, bizarre attempts at flight.

Dad came out the back door. "Thunderstorm brewing," he said. "I've never seen the animals so riled up."

The light breeze we had most evenings had failed entirely tonight, and the air carried a sultry deadness. But the storm didn't come. It rumbled like a faraway train but didn't get any closer.

A ribbon of sky opened up in the west under the layer of clouds, showing the sun already half sunk behind the hills. For an instant, a narrow band of sunset threw gold-pink light on the river and the fields, the kind of light that, if you saw it in a painting or a book, would make you say, "No, no, that's fake; it could never look that way in real life."

Then the sun dropped and the clouds closed up again as quickly as they'd opened. Gradually, the electricity went out of the air. The animals calmed down, and it looked like the storm wasn't coming our way, after all.

Marie found us on the porch and said somebody was here. Dad sent her back in, while he and I went around the house to the front yard. Deputy Jack G. was getting out of his Ford pickup.

He was wearing his uniform, something I didn't often see him do. He was thin-boned and wouldn't ever have any real weight to him, although his shirt was a little too tight around the middle. He came through the gate, nodded at both of us, and asked me how I was doing. He said, "Looks like you had a fire."

I nodded. He raised an eyebrow, but he didn't ask

any questions. From then on, he talked to Dad while I listened and watched.

"I been up to see Leeper again, Dale," he said.

Dad nodded, and he went on.

"Honest to John, that man's dangerous as a drunken fighter pilot right now. I don't want to scare you." He glanced at me. "But the thing of it is, last night when I told him about his boy and again this mornin' when I told him we'd found the body, both times he got mad as a cornered badger. That's why I called early and told you to be careful."

Nobody had told me about that phone call. So that was the real reason Dad was home, I figured.

Jack G. went on. "Now, I been at this job a long time and I seen a lot of different attitudes when you tell people somethin' like this. I seen 'em all. So to see him get mad like that, well, that was a bad sign. He was needin' somebody to blame."

The deputy was smoking a hand-rolled cigarette with one hand and resting his other palm on the top of the revolver on his hip.

"Well, his talk still gave me cause to worry. So I put on this goofy uniform that I don't wear no more'n twice a year—thought that might scare some sense into him—and went back up there a while ago. I got him to talkin' and sure enough, he was sayin' how this never shoulda happened, about how he had no idea there was a raft down here waitin' to drown his boy—things like that. Said you shoulda been more careful. And that he'd 'have to look into it,' as he called it. Well, when he said that, I knew we had a problem."

I felt a wave of fear. Jack G. went on.

"Now, you know the man is slower than December tar, Dale, so I don't know if he took in all my words or not, but I told him to forget all that horsefeathers. That you're as good a man as there is and that the only thing that would happen, should he ever have the least little thought of takin' things into his own hands, is that I'd be back up there and cart him off to jail so fast he wouldn't have time to pack a toothpick or kiss his pet mule bye-bye on the way out. I told him that straight out.

"Now, I mighta made a little headway there, Dale. He calmed down some. But whether he was fakin' it to keep me off his back, I couldn't tell. He's slow, but he's connivin', too. And even a sweenied horse can kick. But I suppose Leeper's been in this town long enough to know I wouldn't hesitate to crack his skull like a black walnut if I had to."

I looked at the deputy as he talked, and remembered the things I'd heard about him. He was a wiry man with wispy, thinning hair, a dark, narrow mustache, and close-set eyes, and he was probably ten years older than Dad. He didn't look tough, especially since he had a crooked smile on his face nearly all the time, but from the stories I'd heard, he wasn't a man to be fooled with. Myself, I'd seen him take action only once, and that was years before at the old dance hall. Two young men with too much to drink started a scuffle without following the unwritten rule that these things be settled outside. Jack G. moved across the hall in about three steps, called them both by name, and said quietly, "Stop it now, boys. Outside."

When they made the mistake, in their drunken state, of taking a few seconds too long to heed that instruction and continued swinging ineffectually at each other, he didn't say another word. Instantly, as if in one motion, he took one step forward, kicked one of them in the knee with his right foot and smashed the other's windpipe with his left elbow. They both hit the floor at the same time. He took a shirt collar in each hand and dragged them outside, where he dumped them on the ground with the little smile still frozen on his face, like he was baring his teeth. While it was shocking to me, it didn't surprise any of the adults who knew the deputy. He had a mean streak, and people thought he might overly enjoy such rough duties, but law-abiding citizens never had a problem with him.

"So, the thing of it is, Dale, I wanted to let you know. I could slap the man in jail in Idaho City if you want me to, but with all those kids and no wife, how's that goin' to work?"

"No, no," Dad said. "Let's hope you don't have to do that."

"Time I left him, he was calmed down, but like I say, that might have been a cover." Jack G. threw his cigarette stub in the grass and smashed it under his heel. I heard the distant beat of the thunder.

"Will you be okay here, Dale?" the deputy asked.

"Sure," Dad said, looking startled at the question. "Sure, we'll be okay."

"Things can happen, you know. You remember old Loomis."

Jack G. glanced sideways at me. "Quiet guy up the Middle Fork. Twenty years ago now, I guess. Shot his neighbor, Old Man Spence, over a fence-line dispute. Gut-shot him and left him to bleed in the field. Wasn't found for two days. He'd tried to crawl to the house. I had to go pick him up. I swear to John, I hope to never see anything like that again."

Dad looked over at me, troubled, I thought, that I was hearing this.

Jack G. held out his hand to Dad, then headed for his truck. "Give me a call if you need me," he said. He turned at the gate and said, "I'll be down to Emmett all day tomorrow. Gotta help my brother move. But I could be reached."

We watched him climb in his truck and drive away. Dad said, "Jamie, I wouldn't worry. We're not going to have any trouble with Arlie." I wasn't so sure. He went on, looking me in the eye and raising his finger, "But let's not worry Mom and Marie with any talk about Loomis or Arlie or anybody. Okay? There's nothing to worry about."

I nodded. And I worried.

ten

It was one of those nightmares where you know it's a dream, but you can't wake out of it. It was about a man who was menacing us in some vague way. It ended with a shotgun blast—only I didn't know who was shot—then I was fully awake, sitting up in bed. My feet hit the floor before I realized that the shotgun blast was actually thunder. My room was bright as day from a flash of lightning and instantaneous thunder, sharp and barbed, like the molecules in the air being split right in two.

An instant later, I heard what sounded like gravel being thrown on the roof, and within seconds the whole torrent crashed down. I got up, shut my window, and went to the kitchen, leaving the lights off.

I expected to find Dad up. He loved lightning storms, and I did, too. I got it from him. Mom told me that when I was small, Dad would take me out on the porch and hold me in his arms to see the commotion when a storm came in, and it never scared me. He'd tried it with Marie, too, but it didn't take with her. Mom and Marie were alike that way. If Marie woke up in a storm, she'd run to Mom's bed, and the two of them would stay right there until it was over.

Dad and I often watched the storms together, day or night. But I didn't find him up tonight.

I even climbed the stairs and opened the window to the north in our narrow attic, to watch the storm light up the curve of the river, the silver metal roof of the sawmill, and Palmer's place, where a light still burned.

I came back downstairs and ended up on the back porch, looking out across the south pasture to the churning river. The huge raindrops froze in place with each flash.

Keno didn't enjoy it like I did. He crouched as far back from the porch doorway as he could get and huddled against the wall, his eyes crazy and his lip curled. I didn't go near him.

The storm hung right over us, rattling the old shake shingles against one another like a drum roll. Water poured off the eaves in streams, and the sloping ground between the house and the outbuildings soon looked like a rippling river of black mud. No wind stirred, and the branches of the trees bowed down, some of them almost to the ground, under the heavy pounding.

A year earlier, when Dad and I were up together watching a storm, we had seen a bolt of lightning hit a tree over a quarter of a mile down and across the river, sending a huge limb crashing partly into the water.

"Only saw that happen once before in my life," Dad

had shouted over the drumming rain. I knew the story. When he was a boy hurrying to get the cows in, trying to beat a storm, lightning had split a tree in half clear to the ground not a hundred feet from him. He let the cows scatter and hunkered in a ditch, soaked, until the storm passed.

In a few minutes, the storm lessened and a light wind came up. Suddenly, I was cold in my pajamas. I came in off the porch and sat at the kitchen table for a time, watching the diminishing storm through the window. I kept wishing Dad was up, and it bothered me that he wasn't. It was lonely without him.

I looked in on Marie. I didn't see how she could sleep through the noise, but her hair was splayed out on her pillow like a golden fan, and she was still breathing deeply and evenly.

I went to the front room and noticed the outside door open a little. It had been hot, but we never left our doors unlocked at night. I stepped to it and was startled to see a figure sitting on the dark porch. I jumped back. Then a distant lightning flash showed me it was Dad. He was sitting on the old davenport with his back to the door, facing out across the front yard and up the Branagan road.

I was hurt to think he was up watching and hadn't come to get me like he always did. I couldn't figure it out.

I started to open the door farther so I could step out, when another weak flash glinted off something lying across his knees. It looked like a rifle!

I gasped and stepped back a little. To make sure, I made my way in the dark to the stairs and felt my way up to the gun rack that hung on the wall about halfway up. With my hands, I searched it. Dad's .300 Savage was in place, as was my .30-30. But Dad's old .30-30, the rifle Mom now used when she went deer hunting with us, was gone.

I stood on the stairs in the pitch-black to calm myself and to think. Dad was watching a lot more than the storm. He was watching for Arlie Leeper. And he didn't want us to know it and worry.

Back in bed, with my thoughts on Dad and Arlie and Dennis, I was restless and couldn't sleep. I tried to figure if I could do anything about Arlie.

I listened to the storm drift north. For a long time, the thunder echoed out of the canyon above the sawmill, up where the river ran wild, a perfect partner with the storm.

eleven

When I woke up Wednesday morning from a troubled sleep, Dad was still asleep. He never slept in this late, so I knew he must have been up most of the night. Mom was sewing at the table. The new milk in the fridge told me Dad must have been up long enough to milk the cow before going to bed, so that must have been near dawn. I checked and the rifle was back in the gun rack.

I didn't say anything about it to Mom, and I wondered if she knew Dad had sat up watching for Arlie Leeper. Surely, she did.

Outside, the grass was wet from the storm. I couldn't find Keno. I went around front and was surprised to find him chained on the porch. We never chained up Keno. Dad didn't like dogs tied up. He must have put him here when he'd finally gone to bed, to warn us if Arlie tried anything.

Keno was dozing, but when he heard me he looked at me pitifully and whined. I unchained him because I thought Arlie wouldn't try anything in the daylight. He was too sneaky for that. Keno licked my hand and shook himself before trotting around back.

Last night's rain started the morning off cool. But it soon burned off and turned muggy, the kind of weather that made movement strenuous. I didn't feel up to much, anyway. I was still tired.

Dad was up before noon but he didn't have much to say except to ask me how I was doing. Marie asked him why he was home from work again today and he said, "Oh, just to keep an eye on things, I guess." I reckoned I now knew what that meant.

After lunch, he kept himself busy outside, maybe so he could have a clear view if Arlie showed up. He worked right through the heat of the afternoon on the hottest job of all, patching the chicken house roof, the sweat dripping off his face like tears. He never asked me to help him—he told me to rest—and it left me feeling useless and restless.

I did try to nap once. While waiting for sleep that wouldn't come, I listened to the cadence of the roofing hammer outside, my mind dealing with concerns lined up in my head like magpies on a fence wire—things like Jack G.'s warnings and my dad sitting up with a rifle across his knees.

There were other thoughts, too—about Dennis, about how we'd treated him, about his thanking me on the river for letting him on the raft, how his face looked as we spilled into the white water, and a dozen other things.

I got up so I could quit thinking, but I didn't feel like doing much. Moving the sprinkler a few times was the extent of my effort all afternoon.

Jerry called to check on me again and tell me the details of his swim to shore, his run to the closest house, and his wild ride with Mr. Carlton. He said the old man got excited and couldn't find his glasses but told Jerry to get in the car, anyway. Jerry tried to get him to slow down on the narrow dirt road, but Mr. Carlton said, "Listen, boy, I drove amb'lance in the first war. I can do 'er. You only got two jobs—to hang on and to tell me if there's a cow in the road." Jerry grabbed the wheel a couple of times, to keep them out of the barrow pit.

Jerry had enjoyed the experience, it sounded like, and enjoyed telling about it. He asked a few questions about the raft ride after he fell off, but I didn't have much to tell.

Later, I was in my room thumbing through a magazine when I heard a vehicle start up. I went to the front room. Mom was at the door watching Dad's truck turn up the Branagan road.

"What's he doing?" I asked.

"Being foolish, I'd say," she said sharply. "He thinks he can talk to Arlie Leeper."

"Oh, man," I said. "Alone?" I stepped to the door with her.

"He didn't want me to go."

I was hurt. "He could have asked me," I said.

"Oh, I guess he'll be all right. It just won't do any good."

Jack G.'s warning came back to me. I hesitated only a second and said, "I'm going." I was out the door like greased lightning. Mom didn't get a word out before I was around the house and getting my bike off the back porch. When I pushed it around front, she was waiting for me.

"Just what do you think you're doing, Jamie?"

"I've got to go up there, Mom."

"But, Jamie . . ."

"No, Mom, I have to go." It was unusual for me to talk back.

She looked at me in surprise, then shook her head like she didn't understand. She opened her mouth to speak, but didn't. She finally nodded and said, "You be careful, Jamie."

I ran the bike to the gate and pushed it through, jumped on, and pedaled hard up the Branagan road.

I didn't see how I would catch Dad, but it was less than a mile to the Leepers' and I couldn't be far behind. When I rounded the bend by the spring, I saw the truck farther up the road, going slow.

I was pedaling furiously and didn't have much time to think, but it came to me how odd it was that it took something like this to cause us to make our first visit to the Leepers' house in the near two years they'd lived here. I hoped Arlie would take it right.

As I came closer, I could see the place looked a lot different than when the Branagans lived here. In good order then, it was now junky and run down. Equipment sat wherever it was last used. A hay rake hunched in a nearby field gone to Johnson grass and thistles, and a rusty harrow brooded a hatch of tall weeds right in the middle of the barnyard.

Dad had driven to the left of the house, around the side to the back door. I went across the yellow lawn to the right. I wasn't sure Dad would want to see me up here, and I didn't want him to send me home. I was breathing so hard from my ride that I had to catch my breath. I leaned my bike against the side of the house and went quietly to where I could peek around the corner.

Dad was standing on the next-to-top step, waiting. He'd lifted Dennis's bike from the truck bed, pushed it over to lean against the cement steps, and was now standing at the bottom of the steps with what looked like a loaf of Mom's homemade bread in his hand.

Soon two little faces appeared like shadows and pushed the ripped screen door open a few inches, then disappeared. Arlie's scowl came into view. His old hat was on his head when he stepped out and pulled the door shut behind him.

"Arlie," Dad started, "I wanted to come up and tell you how sorry I am—we all are—about your boy." He paused, but Arlie didn't answer. "It's a terrible thing. If there was any way to change things . . ."

Arlie looked down from the steps, his face hard, and it was clear as the noonday sun that he didn't like what he was hearing. I wondered if he would start shouting, like he did the other night about his fence. He could have helped my dad feel better about things right now by saying something decent, but I knew better than to expect something like that from Arlie Leeper.

Dad's hand started to reach out with the bread. "My wife wanted you . . ."

But Arlie put up both his hands like a wall, stopping Dad in mid-sentence, his arm still outstretched.

Arlie spoke. "Somebody got my boy killed."

Dad was too shocked to speak. Arlie went on. "That boy of your'n." His voice was a low, sinister hiss I could barely hear from where I peeked around the corner. "He's the one that started the fire with his foolishness. And now he went ahead and got my boy killed."

I pulled back from the corner and pressed my back against the side of the house, not breathing. I felt like I'd had an execution sentence pronounced on me.

I heard nothing, and I peeked around again. Dad was lowering his arm slowly, like a movie in slow motion. Then, suddenly, a high-pitched voice I didn't recognize was shouting, "You stay away from my son, Leeper. So help me, you keep away from my boy."

I didn't know what scared me more—Arlie's piercing accusation or my dad becoming a raving madman.

Dad's hysterical reaction got Arlie's attention, and he took a step back. When he spoke again, his voice was stony and withering. "What'd you think I'd do, kiss you on the cheek for what you done to my boy? You come up and say your little sorry's like that was supposed to change things. Well, I know how folks hereabouts feels about the Leepers, and there ain't nobody sorry—nobody at all."

Dad's voice was closer to the right pitch now, but still shaky, and he said, "My boy is not to blame here, Arlie, nor is Jerry, the other boy. If you want to blame somebody, it will have to be me. I'm the one that encouraged the boys to befriend Dennis."

"Well, then," Arlie said, looking Dad up and down. "Well, then."

Now Dad's tone was pleading, and I hated to hear him sound that way, especially before Arlie Leeper. "We had no idea that raft would get away. We had them tie it up with a rope, made them promise to stay close to shore. But somehow . . ."

Arlie interrupted. "And you was the one that sat there in that boat and pulled your *own* boy up out of that river, now wasn't you? And then you come up here with your pitiful little loaf of bread, like that was to make things just fine."

He spat out the words quietly, but in a menacing way that scared me a lot more than when he blustered and bellowed. His face was grim and hateful, his eyes scrunched up. I could hardly stand to watch.

"Well, it won't work. I know what you done. I know you picked up your own boy and left mine to drown. I know how people would think about pullin' a Leeper out of the water. 'Get the other'n first,' they'd say. 'Then, if there's nothin' else pressin' afore suppertime, maybe we'll take a glance around for the Leeper.'" His words oozed sarcasm and bitterness.

"That's not true, Arlie," Dad said, his voice still wobbly. "That's just not true. We went up and down that river and we never saw your boy at all. Not once. Not before nor after we picked up Jamie."

Completely ignoring Dad's answer, Arlie said, "But a Leeper gets even," his voice now as flat and calm as if he was quoting the price of chicken feed. "You'll see. You'll soon enough see that a Leeper don't just sit by and let it go."

Arlie said something about the deputy that I couldn't make out. Dad stood quiet. I felt like I needed to go and stand beside my dad against Arlie Leeper. But right then Dad made a kind of hopeless gesture with his arms and backed down the steps, sidling toward the truck, never turning his back on Arlie. I stayed put.

When Dad reached the truck door, Arlie called out, "You was always out to get us. First the fire, now this." He was louder now, more his old, loud self. "You even wanted my posts to fix my own fence. And like a fool, I give 'em to you. Well, now you owe me more than money can pay. And you'll soon see . . ." Then, suddenly mute, he stopped and clamped his jaws shut like a trap.

Immediately, Jerry's prophecy about Arlie demanding a reckoning for his posts leaped back to my mind. "You watch . . . ," Jerry had said. It was even worse than that; Arlie was now asking retribution for his boy.

Dad opened the door and got in. He started the

engine. Out the window, he said so quiet I could hardly hear, "Arlie, you can blame me if you must, but you leave my family out of it, or you'll have to deal with me."

Arlie said nothing. He just stood and watched Dad drive away, his face scornful and his arms folded imperiously across his chest, like a powerful emperor triumphant over a foe.

I hated him for what he'd done to my dad. I wanted to step out and tell him to keep his filthy threats away from my dad, but all I did was hide and watch him until he finally went back in his house. Then I slipped back along the side of the house to my bike and coasted down the hill. I felt shaky and scared, now that the moment was past, and I couldn't get away fast enough.

When I got home, Dad was waiting for me at the gate with Mom. He had the truck keys in his hand, like he was ready to start back for me. "Are you okay, Jamie?" he called as I coasted in.

"Yes," I said.

"I didn't know you were up there. Did you hear . . . ?"

"Yes, I heard it all," I said.

Mom had the bread in her hands. She turned to me, "Oh, I'm glad you're back, Jamie. I don't want you up there again. Now, Dale, finish telling me what happened. He wouldn't even take the bread?"

"No. He . . . ," Dad started. "It's not good."

"What did he say?" Mom asked.

"Where's Marie? I don't want her to hear it."

"She's playing the phonograph," Mom said. I could hear "Froggy Went a-Courtin' " coming from the front room. It was one of her favorites—and mine—with its chorus that sounded like "Teemy-time-oh, in the land of Pharoah-Jay-ro."

Dad said, "Evy, listen, Arlie is upset. He's hurting and he's blaming. I want you and the kids to go into town and stay there overnight."

Mom was startled. "What's going on, Dale?" she asked sharply.

"Nothing's going on. I just want to make sure you're not in danger."

"If there's danger," Mom said, "you're coming, too. You're crazy as a pet coon if you think you're staying out here to face that man alone."

Dad took her by the arm. "Listen, Evy. Arlie's all bluff. He's not going to actually do anything . . ."

"How do you know that?" Mom asked. "If you really thought that, you wouldn't be sending us away."

"I guess I don't know for sure. But I do know two things. First, if he does try anything, you and the kids shouldn't be here. That would be foolish. Second, if he tries anything, he can't find the place deserted. There are animals and buildings here . . ."

"Dale, we'll call Jack G. If Arlie threatened you, Jack G. can come and arrest him. All you have to do is ask."

"He's out of town all day today."

"We can call the sheriff up at the county seat."

"It would take hours for him to get down here. Besides, Arlie didn't actually threaten me, so there's not much of a case."

Mom raised her palms in exasperation. "He didn't threaten you?"

Dad hesitated and looked at me quickly before saying evenly, "No, Evy, he didn't threaten me." Mom looked at him hard.

My jaw nearly dropped! Dad couldn't have forgotten Arlie's threatening words: "A Leeper gets even. . . . A Leeper don't just sit by and let it go." Dad had to know as well as I did what those words meant.

But then, in an instant, it was clear as day to me what he was trying to do—protect Mom from worry. I was surprised he would tell less than the full story, but I didn't have much time to think about it.

Dad hurried on, his voice a little sharp. "Evy, I can tell you about it later. But right now, I really think you need to get going before it gets dark."

Mom hesitated. "Well, okay," she said. "I'll need to come back tomorrow to get ready for the funeral."

"Sure, you can come back anytime after daylight," Dad said. He turned to me. "Jamie, you go get Marie ready—get her pajamas and whatever she needs. And you, too. Don't tell Marie anything; I don't want to scare her. I'll call Lois."

"Dad," I said, "I don't want to go. I want to stay with you."

"No, Jamie," Mom said. "You need to come with us."

I started to protest, but Dad said, "Jamie, let's hurry."

I went to do as I was told. I brought the bread to the kitchen and told Marie to put her things in a paper bag and that she was going with Mom to sleep at Aunt Lois's house tonight. "Mom will tell you all about it on the way," I said. "Hurry." She scooted off to her room to get ready for her great adventure while I turned off the phonograph. Dad cranked the phone for the operator while Mom went to get her things together.

We went out to the car. Mom and Marie got in and Dad went to Mom's side. He saw me standing on the other side of the car. "Get in, Jamie. Where's your things?"

I'd made my decision. "I want to stay," I said. I said it calmly. Everybody looked at me. "I told you I wanted to stay here, Dad. I'm old enough to help."

Dad looked at me for half a minute while Mom looked first at me, then at him. She nodded once.

"Okay, son," he said. Mom backed the car out and Dad came over and stood beside me. We waved and watched them go.

"I'm glad you stayed, Jamie," Dad said, "but I want you to keep near me. I need to know where you are all the time."

I agreed, and Dad went on. "I really don't think

Arlie will do anything, but you heard him. He's hurting, and you never know."

We stood for a moment, then Dad looked at the sky. "There's a lot of thunderheads building up, so let's get the chores done. Another storm might hit. I'll milk."

At the granary, I spread a few handfuls of wheat onto the hard ground where the kernels bounced like hail. I watched a moment as the chickens pecked and scratched, and wondered why they felt the need to dig at the ground when the grain was right there in plain sight. It was like their gullets wouldn't work unless their feet were moving.

Back in the house, Dad was putting away the milk when the phone rang. I answered it. It was Mom telling us they were at Lois's house safe and sound, and that they were sending us supper with Uncle Oscar and Jerry.

"They're coming to stay with you tonight," she said.

That was a surprise.

"They want to help. Jamie, don't you and Jerry go doing anything silly. You stay right where your Dad tells you. Promise me."

"We will, Mom," I said. It made me feel better to have Uncle Oscar and Jerry coming. When I told Dad, he was pleased also.

A wind was stirring up, gusting hot and dry. It was overcast now, the sun gone.

When Jerry and Uncle Oscar came we sat in the living room, because it was on the front of the house where we could watch. We ate the fried chicken Mom and Aunt

Lois sent. Uncle Oscar said, "That was larrupin' good." It was one of his sayings. When he ate at our house, he'd say to Mom, "Mighty good truck, Sal."

With Dad sitting where he could see up the Branagan road, we talked as dusk fell. Uncle Oscar rubbed his bald head and asked questions of me, about what had happened on the river. Jerry surprised me by saying he was sorry he hadn't been more careful. I told him we all should have been careful. There was no need for him to take the blame.

By the time we cleaned up supper, it was close to dark. The wind had died down, and it didn't look like the storm was coming our way, although I could hear distant thunder. While we ate, heavy clouds had formed a leaden cover over the valley, holding in the day's heat. Even the crickets sounded lethargic in the mugginess, and Keno lay in a heap by the back porch like he'd been knocked out.

A car came up the river road. We watched carefully, out of sight of the windows, and when it passed by, we could see it was Bill Benbow, who lived another two miles up the road.

Dad asked me to chain Keno out front like last night. He turned on both porch lights and went out and turned on all the other outside lights.

I chained up Keno, much to his displeasure. When I came back in the house, Dad was coming down the stairs, Mom's .30-30 rifle down by his leg, sort of like he was trying to hide it. He stood it in a corner. Everybody stared at him. "We won't need this, of course," he said flatly.

When darkness came, we left off the lights in the house. It made us feel less like we were in a fishbowl. It reminded me of Grandpa's house, where he would sit in the near dark every evening, saving electricity, until it finally got fully dark. Tonight, it was eerie, the four of us sitting in the living room with the only light coming through the open door from the porch. It was bright enough that we could make out the furniture and each other, but I couldn't see the faces clearly.

Dad was in his big chair. Without an invitation, he took a deep breath and started telling the story of our visit to Arlie. He told about Arlie's hard attitude, and about his rejecting Dad's expression of sorrow about Dennis's death. Dad had his hand on the chair arm and rubbed it back and forth as he talked.

"At first, he blamed Jamie. Of course, he didn't know—and I didn't know—that Jamie was right around the corner listening. But when he blamed Jamie, I came near to tearing him in half. That's the only time I 'bout lost my control. I just couldn't have that. I told him if he had to blame anybody, it couldn't be these boys. It would have to be me—for wanting them to be friends with Dennis and for letting these boys out on a raft in the first place. And he seemed to act like he'd now found the real enemy. He glared at me for a long time. That's when I knew we had a real problem here—not just a grieving man, but a dangerous man."

I remembered Arlie looking contemptuous, nodding his head slowly and profoundly, like a brilliant prosecutor in a movie who has just tricked the defendant into a confession of guilt right before the judge and jury.

I felt so sorry for my dad, having to stand there and take that abuse from a maniac like Arlie Leeper.

Dad told about how Arlie made his threat at the end. "Arlie said, 'A Leeper knows how to take care of things. 'Course, I make no threats. The deputy wouldn't like that, would he? But we'll just see how things come out by and by, now won't we?'"

Uncle Oscar shook his head and Jerry made a sound with his breath.

"I never felt so low in my life," Dad said.

Uncle Oscar told him the same things Mom had told him—that it was an accident, that it would do no good to blame himself, that these things just happen.

"I'd sure like to go back and live this week over again a different way," Dad said with a sigh.

Uncle Oscar asked a few questions, and the men talked quietly about Arlie and his ways, and whether he was likely to do anything against us. They agreed that he probably wouldn't, but I thought they might have been saying that partly so as not to worry Jerry and me.

"I guess we'll see what he's like at the funeral tomorrow," Uncle Oscar said. "That may tell the tale."

I listened to the talk, but I didn't say much. I was tired and the corner of the davenport felt comfortable.

When the phone rang just before ten o'clock, it was loud in the dark and I jumped. Jerry was closest and answered it. It was Aunt Lois calling to see how things were going before they all went to bed.

"No problem here," Jerry said. "Quiet as grass growing."

The next thing I knew, I awoke with a start to Keno growling. The other three were already at the door and the front window, off to the side. I jumped up, instantly awake.

"What is it?" I asked.

"Shhhhh. Keno hears something he doesn't like," Dad said. "Stay back. Don't be seen."

Keno sat at the edge of the porch and peered into the darkness, growling slightly, like he wasn't sure. He didn't bark.

"I'll check the back," Uncle Oscar said as he headed for the kitchen.

Dad said, "I'll go upstairs. One of you boys stay here and the other check the side window. But stay out of sight." He went up the stairs.

Jerry made no move, so I went to the south window in the same room, looking out at Marie's playhouse and the row of walnut trees. I couldn't even see their outline, except where faint light from the front porch hit some of the leaves. I had the feeling anyone outside could look in and see me, even if I couldn't see him. It gave me the jitters.

Soon I moved to the dark kitchen, where Uncle Oscar was. Out back, besides the porch light, the two backyard lights were on—one on the front of the storage cellar and one on a pole halfway between the house and the chicken house—and they cast strange shadows, but nothing was moving. The whirring clock said 11:42.

I moved to my room, from where I could see the light on the barn across the creek. The floor above me squeaked as Dad went back and forth to the windows in each end of the attic. It was the only sound; the thunder was gone.

When I got back to the living room, Jerry was standing to the side of the doorjamb, looking out. I asked if he saw anything.

"Naw," he said. "That porch light doesn't do much." He added, "If Arlie Leeper's coming for your dad, he won't just walk up to the door."

Coming for your dad. I repeated it in my mind. The sound made me shudder.

In a minute, he called quietly, "The dog's quieted down."

Keno had moved back onto the porch and lay down. Soon both men came back to the living room and sat down.

"Probably a night creature," Uncle Oscar said.

We sat in the silence for a time before Uncle Oscar spoke again. "Dale, why don't you and Jamie go and rest? Jerry and I will watch, and if we need you, we'll call."

We decided to do shifts. Jerry and Uncle Oscar would rest first and we would wake them up at 3 A.M. to spell us off. Jerry went to lie on my bed and Uncle Oscar on Mom and Dad's. I stayed on the davenport and Dad took the chair that had a view of the Branagan road.

"You can go ahead and sleep, Jamie," Dad said. "You've been through a lot, and there's no need for both of us to stay awake."

I protested that I would keep him company, and he didn't argue, but soon I was nearly dozing.

I awoke to movement. "What?" I said.

Dad was standing over me. "It's after three," he said. "Jerry and Oscar are up. Go get in your bed; you'll sleep better. I'm going to bed, too."

"Any sign?" I asked.

"All quiet," Dad said.

Uncle Oscar was in the chair Dad had vacated, and Jerry was on the other end of the davenport. I got up groggily. On my way to bed, I stopped in the kitchen for a drink. The night was cooler now. When I stepped into my room, I stopped. "Dad," I called sharply, but not very loud. "Come here."

When he came up behind me, I said, "The light's out. The barn light. It was on before. Now it's out." I felt a chill of fear.

Suddenly, all three of them were beside me, looking out my window.

"Oh, oh," Uncle Oscar said.

"Did you turn it off?" Dad asked. "Did anybody turn it off?" Nobody had. "I'm going upstairs." He turned and headed for the stairs, picking up the rifle on the way. "You guys check the other windows, like before."

I checked the kitchen windows and went to the living room. Nothing in sight. I checked on Keno. He was sitting on his haunches looking out into the darkness, but he wasn't growling this time. Uncle Oscar and Jerry joined me and we made the circuit inside the house twice more.

Dad called down in a stage whisper to ask if we could see anything. We told him no. He said he couldn't, either.

Uncle Oscar said, "Maybe the bulb burned out." Maybe. *Or maybe that worthless Arlie Leeper is out there waiting for a chance to hurt my dad,* I thought.

"It's hard to see past these porch lights, Dale," Uncle Oscar said quietly. "What if we turned them all off for a minute?"

"Go ahead," Dad whispered down. I turned off the front light. Uncle Oscar turned off the back porch light, and I heard him step out on the porch where the switches for the yard lights were, then quickly step back in and slide the bolt in the door. The small amount of light we'd had was now all gone and so was the comfort it brought. Now it was black and eerie. I couldn't even see Keno when I knew right where he was, not four feet outside the door.

I stood there, waiting for my eyes to adjust, but it didn't help much. The night was overcast and not even starlight could get through. But when the eyes don't work, the ears work better. I thought I heard something. I snapped the porch light back on, but nothing was to be seen. The light didn't even reach past the edge of the grass. But Keno had heard it, too. He was off the porch now, looking toward the barn. I turned the light back off and called Uncle Oscar softly. He made his way to me in the dark, Jerry right behind.

"I heard something," I whispered. "Keno, too." I was breathing hard.

"Like what?"

"Like a brushing or a rustling. In the grass. Toward the creek."

Uncle Oscar went up the stairs to talk to Dad, where they could overlook the spot. Jerry and I stayed at the door. In a minute, Jerry thought he heard it, but I didn't hear it again. All I could hear now was my heart.

Keno started to growl quietly, deep in his throat.

"Let's go upstairs," I said. I wanted to be near Dad. I shut the door quietly and locked it. We felt our way across the room and up the stairs.

The two men were looking out the north window toward the barn. "I thought I heard a movement out by the creek once," Dad said quietly, "but I haven't heard it since."

We all listened. I hated this.

"It might be a night creature," Dad said.

"Shoot the rifle," Jerry whispered.

"What?" Dad asked.

"Shoot in the air, to scare him away."

Uncle Oscar said, "Jerry, we don't even know . . ."

Jerry cut in, "What can it hurt? If there's anybody there, it might help. We know there's *something* there; the dog's growling."

"I don't like to just shoot," Dad said.

I thought of the story Dad told of the night he'd stood at this window and, as a prank, shot the rifle three times in the air to scare his friends who had come to steal chickens. Sometimes, after a dance, they would come to get a few of our birds, take them home and fry them, then invite Dad and Mom to a chicken breakfast—of their own chickens—at three or four o'clock in the morning. This time, Dad heard them, knew who they were, and waited until they were right beside the house when he opened up with the rifle right above them. One of them, Gordy Porter, let the chickens scatter and cleared the five-foot gate in a spectacular moonlit leap that was a legend in our town.

"What can it hurt?" Jerry asked again.

Dad hesitated a moment while we listened. Then he slowly levered a shell into the chamber and pointed the rifle out the window at the sky. "Better cover your ears," he said.

We all did that, but the two explosions in rapid

succession still sounded like cannon fire in the confined attic. Keno gave a startled yelp at the first one. The sharp and pleasant smell of gunpowder lingered in the still air.

We strained our ringing ears but heard nothing more. Whoever or whatever was out there had either moved on or was just waiting silently in the dark.

twelve

After Dad shot the rifle in the night, we spent a lot of time moving from window to window, looking, listening, turning the lights on and off, and watching Keno. But we never heard another thing. And Keno settled down shortly afterward. We were wide awake for another hour or more, sitting in the living room, talking quietly, listening to the creaking of the house. We were still edgy, and once in a while, one of us would get up and make the circuit to look out all the windows.

We speculated about what we'd heard. Jerry was sure it was Arlie; the rest of us didn't know. I hoped not. I didn't know what I would do if I knew Arlie Leeper was trying to hurt my dad. But something. Something, for sure.

The talk quieted down after a time, and I finally dozed on the davenport. At dawn, I awoke to Dad and Uncle Oscar talking. From their thick voices, it sounded like they'd slept, too. Jerry was asleep on Mom and Dad's bed. Dad and Uncle Oscar went outside and I watched them out my window as they looked around the creek and the barn. Uncle Oscar hauled two hay bales out of the barn and stacked them on the ground, under the light fixture, then climbed up on them. He reached up and turned the bulb. It was still just dark enough that, from my window, I could see the light come on.

Holy creation! I thought. *So it really was Arlie. He loosened that light bulb so he could move around doing whatever he was doing and not be seen.* Then I thought, *Now wait a minute—even Arlie wouldn't be dumb enough to stand under a bright light while it was on, after fussing around and finding something to stand on, and unscrew a light bulb, knowing we might be watching.*

On the other hand, Arlie *was* dumb, so maybe he would. And the fact is that we weren't watching at the moment it went out, so how could we know? He might have chanced it. I had to conclude that Arlie did it. The thought chilled me to the bone.

When Dad and Uncle Oscar came back in, though, they weren't sure. "That bulb wasn't actually loose," Uncle Oscar said. "I hardly touched it and it came on, so maybe it just has a loose filament."

Maybe. I went to the back porch and flipped the switch off and on a half dozen times. The light came on every time. "Looks pretty good to me," I called.

But if Arlie Leeper had been here in the night he was gone now, so Uncle Oscar woke Jerry up and they went home to get some sleep before the funeral. By the time Dad milked and I did the other chores, it was bright morning. In a few minutes, Mom and Marie drove in.

Dad didn't tell them much of what had happened in the night, but he said, "I'm sure we'll be fine in the daylight, Evy. But keep Marie in, anyway, and the doors locked, while Jamie and I get some more sleep."

On my bed, sleep arrived and took me to someplace deep and far away, but not very restful.

I awoke groggy and sweaty in the late morning, stretched out on my bed, still in my clothes. The clouds were still here, and with no breeze at all, the air was muggy and sweltering. August was a hot month, but there were always a few particularly sticky and oppressive days people dreaded, and this was feeling like another of them. I'd be glad when this siege passed.

After a lunch that nobody seemed to much want, we all cleaned up and put on Sunday clothes, except for Marie, who wouldn't be going to the funeral but would stay with a friend. When I was ready, I lay on my back on the lawn out front. I was careful not to get grass stains on my white shirt as I looked up at the sky and waited until it was time to go.

On hot summer days, I liked to watch the thunderheads rise up thousands of feet in brilliant white columns like geysers. They made bizarre forms and shapes—strange creatures, mostly, and odd-looking people. I would lie back and watch and think of eternity, and fancy myself the one and only person for whom the clouds created their effects and for whom the world turned on its axis. But today there was no display—for me or for anyone else—because there was nothing to see in the sky, nothing at all—only flat, solid, monotonous gray.

I heard the deep drone of a huge bumblebee roving lazily in Mom's flowers, but I had no interest in it. My fingers absently scratched Keno's neck as he lay beside me panting, his tongue hanging out nearly to the grass.

His ears went up, and a few seconds later I heard the creak of Arlie's truck on the Branagan road. It was early, but the Leepers were already headed to town. My first thought was to get out of sight. But on second thought, I decided I wouldn't let Arlie Leeper make me hide out in my own yard in broad daylight, and I rolled over to look. Keno barked once and I told him to settle down.

As if already in the funeral procession, Arlie was driving slowly. As he crossed the bridge I thought he looked our way, but I couldn't tell if he saw me in the grass. Suddenly, the truck stopped. One of the little kids jumped off the back and ran toward the yard like his shirttail was on fire. I was too startled to do anything but stare as he stuck a piece of paper under the windshield wiper of the Dodge and ran back to the truck, which was getting underway again even before the kid got himself fully back on. A misty brown dust snake trailed them down the road and stayed hanging in the still air a long time after the truck was out of sight.

A couple of minutes later, I found Dad moving the sprinkler on the other side of the house. "Dad," I said. "You need to talk to the deputy."

He straightened up and looked at me.

"About Arlie," I said.

"There's not much to talk about," he said. "There's no evidence."

"He was here last night, Dad. He must have been."

"Well, maybe. We don't know."

"Pretty likely, I'd say."

"Jamie, that bulb . . ."

"Do we have to wait for him to burn down the barn or shoot you before we—"

"Well, I don't think he'll do any of those things, do you?" He looked puzzled.

"I don't know what he'll do." My voice came out angry. "But he did threaten you. Which you didn't tell Mom."

Dad studied me. "Maybe the funeral will help him come to terms," he said.

I handed him the note. "What's this?" he asked.

"Arlie just had one of his kids deliver it."

YOUR NOT WELCOM AT THE FUNRAL.

Dad read it aloud, then read it again. He turned it over, then read it a third time. "Well . . . ," he said.

"This is what we're up against, Dad," I said. "A madman, telling us what we can and can't do, sneaking around our place in the night, threatening you yesterday."

"Probably one of the kids wrote this," Dad said.

"Oh, cripes, Dad. Who *told* him to write it? Who stopped the truck to let him deliver it?"

Dad just looked at me.

"Do something," I said.

He looked at the paper again. "Maybe the funeral will help him . . ."

"Maybe," I said. "But talk to the deputy, too." I wasn't used to telling Dad what to do, and I was surprised at myself. But with Arlie after us, everything was different.

Dad said, "Don't tell your mom about this note." He pushed it into his pants pocket.

Fine. I didn't care about that. "You have to do something. *Somebody* has to do something." Dad just studied me.

In another half hour, it was time to leave for the funeral. The car was an upholstered oven, even with the windows down, and it was a quiet ride. My mind was occupied, wondering whether something would happen at the funeral to help Arlie see things differently.

As we came past the Big Ranch field, which hid the first dam, a shiver ran down my back. A few minutes later, as we passed where I knew the second dam to be, out across another field, my mind brought up a vivid and disturbing picture of the thundering and deadly cascade.

This was my first trip in the car since the accident. Things looked different somehow, the colors bright, even under a dull sky, the world shining and polished and new.

Gauzy heat waves rose from the road, making it all appear like a dream.

"Is that where they found Dennis?" Marie's question startled me back to reality. The road had come back to the river here, where the horseshoe curve started, and we could see the shallows and the highway bridge still a half mile downstream. That's where Marie was pointing.

Mom answered, "Yes, honey, that's the place."

A moment later, just past the turnoff to the cemetery, a strange thumping was heard. Dad pulled over and stopped. "What is it?" Mom asked.

Dad opened his door and looked back. "Oh, corruption!" he said. "A flat."

"Oh, my," Mom said. "Now we'll be late."

We all got out and looked at the left rear tire, splayed out on the dusty road like a smashed toad.

Dad wasted no time getting the jack from the trunk, then the spare tire, which he held away from his good clothes. He pumped the jack and I squatted and held it in place until it caught under the rear bumper and the car started to rise.

Mom and Marie stood behind us on the road in the heat. It wasn't sunny, but it was bright and the nearest shade was two hundred yards away, in the cemetery, a grassy oasis on the dry brown hillside above us.

"There's Grandpa's car," Marie said, pointing at Grandpa's green Plymouth coupe, parked behind the toolshed in the cemetery.

Since his retirement from ranching, Grandpa had

been the cemetery caretaker. He was old but still strong, and he could always get a yelp out of me when he squeezed my knee with his long fingers, now age-splotched and shaky, but still powerful. He watered, mowed, trimmed, and kept the cemetery looking nice—especially, I thought, around Grandma's grave. Sometimes when we drove by, we'd catch a glimpse of Grandpa's head of thick white hair moving among the tombstones like a ghost. Today, I couldn't spot him. But his car was there, so I knew he was up there to make sure everything was in order before the people came to bury Dennis.

Down by the river, near the electric pump that pushed river water up a pipe to the cemetery grass, I saw a brown bird, a killdeer. He hopped quickly from rock to rock, always watchful and on the lookout for danger—ready to trick an enemy away from his nest by dragging a wing.

Dad was hurrying, but it was slow going because of his good clothes. He had the tire off now. Marie came over and wanted to hold the lug nuts for him. There wasn't much I could do but hand him the lug wrench at the right time. But I wanted to help.

Beside Grandpa's Plymouth was Ole Swensen's old pickup. Ole was the night watchman at the sawmill and dug graves on the side. He had dug all the graves in our cemetery for thirty-five years or more—even when the three Collins boys were killed in a car wreck in Dad's youth and Ole had to work by lantern light to get all three graves ready in time. Help had been offered, then and at other times, but Ole was protective of his work and wouldn't accept it. He drank up all his pay, they said, but he took pride.

Ole would have Dennis's grave all ready by now. He'd stay out of sight, smoking behind the toolshed when the people came for the burial, biding his time until they left. Then he'd pick up his shovel and cover over the first Leeper ever to be placed in the midst of the Hansons, Frys, Shelleys, Zimmers, Faulls, Quinns, and other old-time families of our valley.

"Okay, let's go," Dad said as he quickly levered the jack handle and let the car down. He lifted the flat tire into the trunk, and we all got back in the car, which was now hotter than ever.

We had barely started out when I asked, "Did Arlie do this?"

"Do what?" Mom asked.

"Do something to our tire?"

In the front seat, Mom and Dad looked at each other like they'd never thought of that. Dad said, "Oh, I doubt it," but his answer was hesitant and his voice unconvincing.

thirteen

We crossed the river bridge, dropped Marie off at a friend's house near the old dance hall, and drove on through town—past Jerry's house, the school, Uncle Oscar's store, and on across the canal and railroad tracks. The town looked nearly deserted. Instead of taking the main turnoff to the Ladies' Club Hall—where funerals, church on Sundays, and Friday night movies were held—Dad turned on a side road that ran behind Foutz's garage and came up to the side of the hall.

Backed up to the side door was the hearse, its deep black surface richly waxed and gleaming. A light coating of road dust was beginning to dull the luster. Our passing would add another layer.

Idling in the shade of the building beside the open back door of the hearse was the man from the funeral home in Boise, a thin stranger in a black suit. He was wiping his shining bald head with a handkerchief. A second, younger man with hot red cheeks sat at the wheel of a vehicle parked across the road, a black Cadillac limousine with the driver's door open. He had one foot on the ground, and he was smoking and listening to music on the radio. Johnny Cash's deep voice sang about walking the line.

Not one parking spot was left beside the building.

Around front, a clump of people stood and others sat on the steps. At first, I thought they were delaying their entrance, since the hall was bound to be suffocating on a day like this. Then I realized, from the number of cars, that the hall must be full and these people couldn't get in.

"This is a funeral-going town," Mom said, "but I didn't expect this kind of turnout. Of course, with the sawmill closing for it . . ."

"The sawmill closed for the funeral?" I asked.

"Yes, at noon," Mom said. Dad found a parking space nearly back out to the highway and turned off the motor.

I said, "But Arlie doesn't work at the sawmill."

"I got a notion maybe people feel bad," Mom said. "About more than Dennis dying, I mean."

I looked at her, not comprehending.

"About how the Leepers didn't fit in, weren't accepted," she said.

As we approached the hall, I could hear piano music from inside. As we came up on the steps, people turned to look at me. Nobody said much, but they nodded, and one of the women reached out to touch my arm.

We looked in through the open double doors. There were rows and rows of people in place, facing away from us. Pastor Soter was seated at the front, fanning himself with a piece of paper. Behind him was the club hall kitchen, where the Leepers would be, behind a curtained doorway.

Seated right before us, in the back row, was Mrs. Iker, my first- and second-grade teacher. She glanced back and saw us and came out. She squeezed me close against her silky black dress and patted my back, the way people pat a baby. When she let me go, tears rimmed her eyes.

Two or three of the men on the steps made a point of standing up and shaking Dad's hand solemnly. I thought it meant something.

Maybe that's why all these people are here, I thought, *to support my dad.* I watched him. He nodded as people greeted him, but he didn't say much, and he sure wasn't his normal, friendly self. I figured he was more worried about Arlie than he could cover up.

I could feel heat pouring out of the hall from all the people packed inside. Mrs. Iker's husband, Babe, came out and ushered Mom to his seat. He stayed with us and talked about how hot it was inside. "Ain't exactly a glacier breeze out here, either," he said.

I was surprised at how many schoolkids I could pick out. It looked like most of our eighth-grade class was here. And I picked out Jerry, sitting with his folks in the middle of the hall.

At the sad old piano with the two broken keys that flopped noiselessly up and down, Mrs. Carter was playing the various segments of hymns she used for prelude music every Sunday at church, running them all together as a medley. Just when you'd get to feeling the flow of one, she'd move to another. Phrases came to me:

". . . Angel faces smile . . ."

". . . Here's my heart, O take and seal it . . ."

". . . The powers of hate o'erthrowing . . ."

". . . Me for the harvest, Lord, prepare . . ."

I'd heard Mrs. Carter play these same tunes every Sunday for years. You'd think she'd have memorized them by now, but she still squinted intently at each note through the bottom half of her bifocals, her narrow nose elevated like a dog pointing a pheasant.

Even from the doorway, the funeral scent, heavy and sweet, assaulted my nose. The smell of flowers in large bouquets inside a building, especially in the heat, was overpowering and unnatural to me and reminded me of decay. And there were lots of flowers here today. Immediately, the smell brought to mind Grandma's funeral of almost three years before, my only funeral until now. We'd come early with my cousins and aunts and uncles to look at Grandma before we took our places in the kitchen. I recalled my surprise at how much Jerry had cried that day.

Aunt Vi stroked Grandma's hair a long time and kissed her. Planning not to look at her, I did. Dad didn't. He wanted to remember her alive.

I was determined not to look at Dennis today, in his open casket up front.

I turned back from the door and spotted Jack G. coming toward us in the street. He was in his uniform again. I went off the steps and out to meet him. He noticed me and nodded. I stopped as he got close enough and said, "Deputy, you have to do something." It made me nervous to have to speak up to Jack G.

He stopped and looked at me, surprised. I went on. "Arlie came around our place last night. Or we think he did."

"What'd he do?"

"Well, we're not sure," I said. "But we know he's upset."

"And you want me to do something?"

"Yes, sir."

"Like what, boy?" he asked.

"I don't know," I said. "Tell him to stop."

The deputy had his normal smile on. "The minister told me Leeper was all riled and makin' noise about if you folks'd be here."

"He told us to stay away," I said. "Sent us a note."

"He did?" Jack G. shook his head. "Well, the thing of it is, Soter got him calmed down, so I didn't go in and talk to him. If he acts up, I swear to mercy I'll do that and more. But he's a sneaky type, and I can't watch him all the time."

He looked at me closely and said, "So just be careful." He moved on, leaving me more worried than ever. Jack G. wasn't going to do anything.

Dad was sitting on the steps when I got back to the hall. I watched from the doorway as Mrs. Carter finished with a flourish, scraped back the bench, and went to sit in the front row.

Pastor Soter stood and strode toward the podium. He had a limp, and it slowed him down some, but he still moved pretty fast for a big man. He was perspiring heavily in his robes.

The pastor was from Georgia, and he talked slow. In his pleasant, low voice, he expressed his pleasure—though I think he meant surprise—at the large crowd. He gave a prayer, then said, "I've asked Hannele Frey, one of the schoolteachers, to tell us about Dennis's life." He sat down again, dabbing at his forehead and cheeks with the hem of his robe.

Mrs. Frey stood from her seat in the front row and started to speak, her clipped Finnish accent a contrast to the pastor's slow drawl. "When Pastor Soter asked me to tell about Dennis today, I realized how little I really knew about the Leepers.

"When the family moved here, Dennis came into my classroom. He was such a quiet boy. If only we had known him better."

She hesitated and looked at the floor, her face pained, two fingers pressed to her lips like a smoker. I remembered, from the sixth grade, how she would make this same gesture when she was upset over something in class.

She got control of herself and went on. "When Dennis came to us, I learned that his mother had died a few months before."

I hadn't known that. I knew Dennis had no mother, but I hadn't given much thought to what had happened to her. I had assumed divorce, since it seemed unlikely that any woman could tolerate living with Arlie Leeper for long.

She paused again. "I don't know," she said at last, "if this is the right thing to say." She glanced over her shoulder at the curtained doorway to the kitchen. "And I don't want to cause Mr. Leeper any extra pain."

Mr. Leeper. It sounded odd to me.

"But what I want to say is that some of us didn't accept Dennis or any of the Leepers very well, did we? We kept them at a distance, didn't we?"

Mrs. Frey ended a lot of her sentences in class with questions she didn't necessarily expect anyone to answer out loud. But if I'd been in her classroom right now, I would have quickly raised my hand and asked *her* a few questions: "Mrs. Frey, don't you see how the Leepers are, how they don't do their part? Don't you see how my dad tries to be a good neighbor, but Arlie Leeper treats him like dirt?" But we weren't in the classroom, and she certainly didn't expect anybody to speak up here.

She went on, her accent deepening as she fought her emotions. She told how we never gave Dennis, and the Leepers in general, a chance to be real members of our community.

I suspected Mrs. Frey was going beyond what the pastor had asked of her. His face showed no concern, however, and she soon moved on to what she was supposed to do—tell Dennis's place of birth and such.

I looked around the hall, at the backs of people's heads. I noticed that the young undertaker never came in the building. But the other one, the thin, older one, now sat on a folding chair just inside the open side door. In his white shirt sleeves, he was the boniest man I'd ever seen.

His thin fingers toyed absently with a ring of keys. I wondered how many people this man had buried, and what mundane thoughts he was thinking right now in the midst of mourning people whose tears he couldn't feel.

I looked back outside at Dad, still sitting on the steps, leaning forward with his elbows on his knees and his chin cupped in his hands.

Before Mrs. Frey sat down, she closed with "I wish we had treated Dennis differently. All he wanted was to be somebody, didn't he?" *Be somebody?* I'd never thought of a Leeper wanting to be somebody.

Mrs. Frey sat down, and Mrs. Carter started up again, this time a sad, slow tune, but I wasn't hearing much of it. I had too much to think about. I went and sat down on the steps, a few feet from Dad.

The deputy couldn't lock Arlie up forever, and Dad couldn't sit up every night with the .30-30 across his knees. What if the funeral didn't soften him, as Dad hoped, and sooner or later he made good his threat about getting even? I knew he was capable of it.

When Mrs. Carter's music died away, I stepped to

the door again. At the front, the pastor wiped his sweaty forehead with his fingertips and started the funeral sermon.

"My friends, we've lost a fine young man. But one thing we can be sure of, and we must make it clear right at the start. The Lord is in charge. He makes no mistakes. No sparrow falls without his knowledge. And Dennis Leeper goes home to him who willed it."

The pastor walked over next to the casket. "Sometimes," he said, a little too loudly, "sometimes, in our pain, we try to make sense of tragedies by placing blame." I looked back out the door at Dad, who raised his head, listening.

"But let there be no bitterness, no hate, no blaming. Mortals cannot argue with the will of God, though we may not always understand."

I saw now what the pastor was up to. He was trying to send a message to Arlie Leeper, and I loved him for it. I hoped Arlie was listening.

Pastor Soter talked on about the love of God, the glorious resurrection, and Dennis living with Jesus forever. He warmed to his subject, using his hands, his voice taking on power.

I prayed as I listened. But I didn't pray for Dennis. I prayed for Arlie. For him to hear, to change, to accept, to let it go, to leave my dad alone.

And as I prayed in my heart, Arlie's face came to the narrow gap in the curtained doorway at the front. He looked different all cleaned up, with his hair combed, but his eyes still smoldered. I felt he was still looking for me, for Dad, for Mom. Involuntarily, I shifted slightly to the side of the doorway.

I looked at that face and realized something: no one was going to take care of this problem. Not Dad nor Jack. G. nor anybody else, not even God.

And in the next few moments, I slowly came to another new thought: that I had it in my power to take care of it myself.

It was now as clear as a cold winter sky to me. Right here and right now, I, Jamie West, could take care of it, and would have to take care of it. I'd have to stand up and do something—call on people for help, tell them Arlie was after us, tell them anything. I didn't know what I would say, but I knew something had to be said and that it was me, and me alone, who had to do it. I had to do it for my dad.

My heart was pounding. I felt like you feel when somebody's head smashes into your stomach in a game at recess. I couldn't concentrate on the pastor anymore, but I did catch something about Jerry and me not being taken because there was still something on earth for us to do.

Maybe he was right about that. I knew for sure what I had to do, and it had to be done soon.

I looked at Jerry, who sat with arms folded, staring at his feet stretched out under the seat in front of him. Little did he know what was coming.

Arlie's face was gone from the curtains, and the pastor sounded about ready to finish. My feet didn't want to move, but the time had come, and I stepped through the doorway. I moved slowly to my left along the back wall, going around several people standing there, ignoring their curious eyes. I waited in the back corner until the pastor said amen. At that instant, while he gathered himself before announcing the rest of the meeting, I started forward.

I noticed heads turn my way, row by row, but I didn't look at any of them. The thin undertaker was right in front of me against the wall, watching me intently from behind the piano, his pale eyes fully open for the first time.

I'd have to pass right by the casket. I looked away.

I was nearly to the front before the pastor noticed me, because he was wiping his forehead again. When his arm came down, his jaw dropped open and his eyebrows arched into sudden question marks, because there I was, before his eyes and before the Lord, standing up in the midst of the congregation.

fourteen

"Excuse me, Pastor," I said weakly.

The pastor took a small, hesitant step toward me. "Jamie," he said. I took a breath and said, "I'm sorry, but I have something to say." My voice was shaking. I'd never seen anybody interrupt a pastor before.

His eyes were wide and surprised. He froze in place, then made a small, accepting gesture with his hand toward me.

My hands were shaking, and I made fists to make them stop.

There were so many faces! In the back, Mom leaned forward like she was ready to stand up, and the confusion on her face told me she thought I'd lost my senses. Dad had come in off the steps and was standing in the doorway. Others from outside—including the deputy, who wasn't smiling now—were joining him and peering in. Every eye, every single eye was on me.

"I have to tell you all something. It's . . . it's about Arlie Leeper."

The silence reached to the moon and back. No one breathed, it seemed. The only movement was out of the corner of my eye, behind the pastor, where the curtains suddenly split open and Arlie Leeper's face looked through. I dared to turn and look at that hard face and those hard eyes and I fumbled. "I . . . I, well . . ." I didn't know how to say that Arlie was after us.

I turned back and my eyes fell on Mrs. Frey, staring up at me. And her question rang in my head: "All he wanted was to be somebody, didn't he?"

That question circled round and round in my mind, like a hawk looking for prey. The people must have thought I'd been struck dumb. But still, no eye blinked, no knee jiggled, no hand fanned the hot air. They had all turned to stone before my eyes.

Finally, Mrs. Frey's question seeped into the inner seams of my mind, and an idea boiled up—simple, clear, and perfect. I knew what I had to say.

I found my voice again. "Well, it's not really about Mr. Leeper. It's about his boy. What you all need to know, and especially what Mr. Leeper needs to know . . ." I paused. I had to be careful. I spoke a little louder now to be sure Arlie heard.

"The pastor says the Lord came down and took Dennis. I don't know about these things, but I know Dennis made his own choice that day. I know Dennis gave his life for me."

The silent curtains jerked open a fraction wider.

"See, what happened when we went over that second dam, we grabbed a couple of cans out from under the raft. Then mine was ripped away in the force of the river, and I went under. I was sure I would drown. I swallowed a lot of water and felt myself blacking out." My voice was strong now.

I wouldn't look at Arlie again, but I hurried on, trying my best to tell it like Mom would tell it.

"Then, a can suddenly came into my hands. Dennis was right there, right against me, and I felt him push his can against my chest real hard, no mistake about it. And then he was gone. He must have tried to hold on. But he was just suddenly gone."

I couldn't believe what I was doing, and I couldn't look any longer at the astonished faces. I picked a straight and true mortar line in the stones of the far wall to keep my eyes on.

"I held on to the can and came up long enough to get another breath or two. The water was real powerful, and I lost that can, too. I went under again, but I guess it kept me up long enough for the men in the boat to see me. That's the last thing I remember until I was in the boat."

My eyes caught Jerry's for a moment, staring hard, but I turned quickly away. I was feeling strong, and I went on.

"I thought people ought to know—and Mr. Leeper especially—that Dennis gave me that can. That's what I wanted to say."

There. Was it enough? But even while I tried to decide, the words still came. I said, "I'm sorry not to tell anybody sooner. But I was ashamed. I was ashamed that

Dennis offered me his can and I took it, never worrying about anybody but myself.

"I hope Mr. Leeper will forgive me."

I started slowly down the side aisle toward the back. I'd gone but two or three steps when there was a slight collective sigh in the room.

Then I heard a sound I didn't know was part of any funeral. Somewhere in the back, someone started clapping. In a moment, a few others joined in. It made me stop and look around. Starting small like that, it unfolded and rolled forward like a thunderstorm, as everybody in the room let their feelings out through their hands.

It filled me with shivers, so I couldn't move. The sound brought the skinny undertaker half up out of his chair like he'd been struck.

It wasn't the loud, raucous kind of clapping, like at the summer rodeo or the town dances. It was smooth and calm, like the sound of a waterfall, and it held steady for a long time, bouncing off the rock walls of the old hall, before finally fracturing and shriveling and vanishing like it never happened. I thought I would never hear such a sound again as long as I lived.

The applause had stopped me right beside the casket, and I found myself looking at Dennis. His face was chapped and red from the sun and the water. His broken old glasses were gone, of course—washed away. I'd never before seen him without them.

The empty grin he always had in life was gone, too.

The funeral people had tried to put a smile on him that wasn't his, and it just made him look sad. He had a broad scrape they'd tried to cover with powder and rouge down one side of his cheek—from where the raft fell down on us, I guessed. And he was clean for once. With no dirt smudged on his face, it didn't look like Dennis.

My last view of him was blurred by sudden, sharp tears that ran down my cheeks in a rush. I'd never before seen anyone my age dead.

Surprised and embarrassed, I had to escape. The side door was closest. I passed the seated undertaker. The other one from outside had come to the door, perhaps to see what the commotion was. I brushed past him.

I moved quickly along the side of the hall toward our car, wiping my face. I knew I didn't want anybody asking me questions when the meeting ended. As I hurried away, I could hear the pastor's voice, but I could no longer make out the words.

From the overcast sky, a sudden gust of wind splattered a few hard raindrops on the shiny black hearse, with a sound like someone throwing a handful of gravel. The rain ended after that one jiggerful, leaving pockmarks on the dusty hood.

fifteen

The layer of clouds had thinned some now, letting more light through, and there was a hot wind gusting and stirring up dust. I sat on the front step at Jerry's place, thinking back on all the funeral processions I'd watched from this same spot.

For as long as I could remember, my folks had dropped me off at Jerry's while they went to funerals, and since he lived right beside the highway, he and I would watch the cars go by on their way to the cemetery.

He was out at the corner of the yard right now, leaning on the fence and looking up the highway.

"Here they come," he called. I looked, but from the step I couldn't see anything yet. So I absently counted the dandelions in the lawn and remembered one early summer when Aunt Lois had paid the two of us a penny for each one we dug out—as long as we got their roots down deep. This time of year, the broad-leafed plants lay flat, but I identified seven of them slyly nestling down, pretending to be grass.

Looking up again, I could see the hearse coming along slowly up by Uncle Oscar's store, and the other cars stretched out behind. The afternoon glare made their headlights look pale and washed out, and the heat waves from the road turned the procession into a ghost caravan floating on a shimmering sea. It would be another few seconds before they reached us.

I thought back on the funeral. When I'd hurried from the hall, I'd gone to wait at the car. Mom had reached me first and put both arms around me, bending my head to her shoulder. Dad came and joined his arms around us both for a long moment. He had the softest and most wondering look I'd ever seen on a man's face.

Soon people started pulling out in their cars. The hearse hadn't come by yet, but we got in and started off, too. I didn't want to face anyone, so I asked to be dropped off at Jerry's, and I knew his folks would bring him there, too. The traffic moved us along until we were out onto the highway, where Dad pulled over beside Foutz's garage. He got out and opened the trunk, took out the flat tire, and carried it over to lean against the wall at Foutz's, under the "We Fix Flats" sign.

When he got back in the car, Dad turned and looked at me. "How are you doing, Jamie?"

"I'm tired."

"You've been through a lot," Mom said from the front seat. She reached back and patted my knee. "That must have been so hard, what you did today. I couldn't believe it when you stood up. But I was so proud."

The deputy's pickup was in front of us now, first in line. Then came the hearse, with the bony undertaker behind the wheel. Next, the Cadillac limousine for the family, driven by the younger mortuary man. The kids were in the back, Arlie in the front, his elbow out the window. It was strange—the Leepers riding in a limousine.

Jerry came back and sat down on the steps beside me. "Let's count," he said. We always counted.

"Three . . . four . . . ," Jerry started his count. It looked like it would be a long one, even though some people who went to a funeral didn't go on to the cemetery.

I closed my eyes a moment. It had been a long night and a longer day.

"Seventeen . . . eighteen . . . ," Jerry counted aloud as the vehicles came slowly by.

The slowness of the procession made the occasional cars going the other way seem to whiz by even faster than usual. Probably Boise people on their way to a weekend at Payette Lakes, ninety miles upriver.

"Thirty. That's a lot. Who'd have thought Dennis Leeper would turn out to be a hero," Jerry said without inflection.

Jerry was starting on me, as I knew he would.

He never took his eyes from the line of cars, but

counted silently with his fingers for a while. I loosened my tie. The wind was dying down.

"There's the last one with lights on," Jerry said. "Forty-two." Four other cars followed, but they weren't anybody we recognized. The way they crowded up, they were likely highway travelers caught behind the string, probably amazed that anybody would merit such a big funeral in a puny town like this, and probably cussing, too, at being held up.

"Plus my folks and yours," I said.

"Oh, yeah, forty-four." We sat silently and looked across the river at the dust rising and blowing along the dirt road from the highway turnoff to the cemetery. The hearse and the other lead cars were now visible as they turned up the steep cemetery turnoff. There wouldn't be enough parking space, that was for sure. The last drivers would have to pull to the side of the road near where we changed the tire and walk up.

"Forty-four's a record, isn't it?" Jerry asked. "Unless maybe Old Man Clarkson had more."

"I don't know." Mr. Clarkson was one of the early town founders. I was too young when he died to know from observation how big his funeral was, but the town still talked about how people had come from as far away as the county seat.

Grandma's was a big funeral, too. As an early settler, lots of people knew her. Also, she was respected as the founder of our church, because she'd persuaded people to find a pastor to start a church in Union, and Pastor Soter had agreed.

I thought Glennie Glen's was likely bigger than Grandma's or Mr. Clarkson's, but it was too long ago to be sure, so I didn't mention it. I was nine or ten years old when Glennie was working on a logging crew for the summer, and a log crushed his head against the loader. It was this same time of year—the last Friday of summer vacation, to be exact—and was to have been his last day at work. Even though I didn't go to the funeral, I heard all about it. I remember the day because the high school in Emmett, where Glennie was to start his senior year, met for classes the next Tuesday morning, right after Labor Day, and closed down at noon for the funeral. Glennie had been athletic and popular, and lots of students and teachers came.

"Wow. A Leeper with a funeral this size," Jerry said, shaking his head.

"Pretty amazing," I said.

"You didn't act amazed that he was a hero." He was boring in now.

"Of course I was, Jerry. Why do you think I didn't tell anybody sooner?"

"I wish I knew." He was looking at me hard now.

"Well, now you know. I explained all that at the funeral. I was ashamed."

He wasn't going to let up, I knew that. After a moment, he stood and went inside. He soon came back out with two tall glasses in his hands.

"Ice water," he said, and set my glass on the step. I picked it up. The ice cubes made faint clinking sounds against the side of the glass and streams of tiny bubbles escaped. Jerry finished his water, turned, and set the glass down on the step beside me. He stood right in front of me so I had to look up at him.

"All right," he said, his voice hard, "since it's the day for making peace with the Leepers, I'll take my turn. I was rotten to Dennis most of the time. I admit it. And I'm not proud of it. But I have to say, if he was still alive, I'd probably do it again. That's how I am; that's how he was. So that's that."

Jerry paused. He took a big breath and stepped in closer. "But Dennis Leeper never could have done what you said he did, Jamie. Anybody would know that kid could never be a hero. Not in ten years. Not in a million years. You saw him at the flume and you saw him on the raft—how he gave up both times and sat there like a headless chicken."

"I told you what happened, Jerry," I said. "People have to accept that."

"Come on, Jamie." His voice had a sharp bite to it. "Anybody else you'd want to name, but *never* Dennis Leeper. *Never.*" He spat in the grass and waved both hands in the air dismissively.

I finished my water in one long swallow that hurt my teeth, and set the glass carefully beside Jerry's on the step.

I took a deep breath and stood up, at the same time

quickly putting a foot behind Jerry's ankle. It wasn't fair with him totally off guard, but I pushed him hard on the chest. He pitched back and hit the grass with a thud.

"What in . . . ?" he yelped.

"Don't say it didn't happen, Jerry." My voice was mostly calm, each word distinct and crisp. I stood over him, fists clenched in case he wanted more, while he stared up at me with wide eyes like he was seeing someone he didn't know. "Not to anybody. Not ever."

I knew Jerry could have stood up and beat me silly if he'd wanted to, and if he hadn't been so shocked. But I didn't care. Right now, I just didn't care. I would stand by what I did, no matter what it cost me.

"I told my story. That's how it is. That's how it has to stay. Don't you go and ruin it."

It was the first time in my whole life I'd ever gotten the best of Jerry, pushing him down like that, and I suppose the moment should have given me pleasure. But in fact, something was hurting inside.

He moved like lightning and took me down in a tackle around my legs, landing me on my back. I hated it when he did this. He sat on me and pinned my elbows and talked quietly.

"Jamie, you're crazy. You're out of your mind. I know why you're doing this. And everybody else will, too. But don't pretend to me that it's truth you're telling. Not to me. I know better."

"Just get off," I said, turning my face away.

He was mad. "Do you think those people clapped

their hands back there 'cause they believed what you were saying? Just ask them. Ask anybody. Of course they didn't. I clapped as hard as anybody, and I didn't believe a word of it. Not a stinking word. To help out, that's all. That's why we did it. Just to help out. We did it for the same reason you told your stupid story—to convince Arlie."

His face was just a foot away. "That's okay, that's fine, it was probably the right thing, what you did, and what we did. Maybe it will work out fine with Arlie, he's dumb enough. But the rest of us—don't start asking the rest of us normal people to believe it was a true story you told."

I was dumbstruck at his harsh words, and I stared at his face for a long time. I had a terrible, terrible fear that he might be right about people not believing, and I couldn't stand it.

He let up the pressure on one arm slightly and with a sudden twist and a furious burst of strength, I threw him off. In all the years, I'd never managed it before.

He hit his head slightly on the corner of the steps, and it shocked him. He knelt there and touched his hair with his fingertips and looked at them several times, looking for blood, but there wasn't any. "Geez, Jamie," he said quietly.

I stood up quickly, startled at what I'd done, and said, "I told you to get off." It sounded stupid, but I didn't know what else to say. Finally, I added, "And don't ever hold me down again. We're through with that."

I didn't know what he might do, so I stood there

while he looked up at me, wide-eyed. He finally shook his head and waved a hand. Without another word, he got up and went into the house, knocking over one of the glasses with his foot as he went by. A cube of ice made a tiny, sharp snap and split into two pieces on the step.

Now that it was over, I was breathing hard and shaking a little. I sat down on the step again for a long time with my head on my knees, and watched the spilled ice melt on the hot cement until nothing was left but a puddle.

Then I stood up and walked around behind the house. I passed Uncle Oscar's workshop at the back of the garage. There sat the power saw Jerry and I had used one day a few years back when his folks were gone. We'd been cutting scraps of wood and my left thumb slipped into the whirring blade. I still had the scar.

Jerry had been kind. He'd led me, dripping blood, into the house to bandage my wound, then laid me on his bed and raised my feet—to prevent shock, he said. He'd read it somewhere.

I went on past the garden to the small barn where Jerry's folks used to keep a cow. It was dark and musty inside. In a corner, I put my forearm up against the rough wall to lean my head on.

Crying wasn't something I did often, but today I made up for lost time.

sixteen

When I finished in the barn, I came back and stood by Jerry's garage, looking out toward the cemetery. Jerry wasn't anywhere to be seen.

I couldn't get his words out of my mind. What if he was right? What if, in spite of the hand clapping and all that, people didn't believe me? What if Arlie didn't believe me? What if I had only made things worse instead of better? I was feeling sick about it.

Dust was rising on the river road, and I wondered who was coming back already. Whoever it was was coming like a blue streak. The wind had died down. The vehicle reached the highway and turned my way. It looked like Jack G.'s pickup. He was known for fast driving, and he came across the highway bridge at a good clip. As he came closer, he slowed down and turned in to Uncle Oscar's without signaling. He turned around sharply, facing the road again, sliding a little in the gravel as he came to a stop with the passenger door next to me.

I was startled to see Mom get out. "Jamie," she said, and stepped over and hugged me. Jack G. started up again and headed to the highway while Mom looked at my face. I knew she could see I'd been crying.

"Where's Jerry?" she asked.

"Inside," I said. "What's going on, Mom?"

She thought I was talking about Jack G. "He's going to pick up Marie from Margaret's."

"I mean, why are you here? Where's Dad?"

"Jack G. sent him home."

"What?" I said.

"Jack G. caught up with us at the cemetery and said we ought to go on home. Your dad agreed to drive himself home if Jack G. would bring me over here with you and Marie. So we could stay here tonight, you know, in case . . ."

"But isn't Arlie okay now?"

"What do you mean?"

"Well, after what I said at the funeral, isn't Arlie okay now?"

"We didn't get close to him, Jamie. Didn't dare. So I don't know."

I was thinking about what Jerry had said. "Do you think . . . ? Did people . . . ?"

Mom looked at me.

I said, "What if Arlie didn't believe me, what I said at the funeral?"

Mom looked down. "I don't know, Jamie." Her voice quiet, she said, "I hate to see you hurting. You did a hard thing today. Right or wrong, it took a lot." She wiped her eyes. "What you did, it might not have been the only way or the best way. But it came from your heart, and it just might be the bravest, most loving thing I ever saw."

We stood another moment.

"I didn't know what else to do," I said.

"I know," she said. "But you did fine. You gave a gift today, and sometimes there's pain in the giving." She kissed her fingertips and reached up to touch my cheek softly with the kiss.

After a moment, I said, "I need to be with Dad. He shouldn't be over there alone."

"Jack G.'s going over as soon as he brings Marie back."

"I'm going with him."

Mom hesitated only a moment. "Your dad figured you'd want to come and said if you did, to let you."

That made me feel good, to know Dad wanted me to be with him.

The timing was perfect. Jack G. pulled back off the highway and stopped beside us.

I stepped over and opened the door for Marie. "Okay, Jamie," Mom said. "You go ahead. We'll be fine here with Jerry until Oscar and Lois show up."

I climbed in beside Jack G. He had his quirky smile on, as always.

"All right, Slim," he said as he put the truck in gear. "Let's scoot on out of here." I waved at Mom and Marie as we started off.

Jack G. turned north and headed up through town.

This route was longer, but I figured he might not want Arlie to see him go by if we went on the cemetery road.

I was glad to be going home to be with Dad. And I felt good being with Jack G., even if we were speeding through town at a rate that would have earned anybody else a speeding ticket.

To test out what Jerry had said, I turned to Jack G. "What about . . . uh . . . how's Arlie Leeper doing?"

"How's he doin'?"

"Yeah, I mean, is he okay? Since the funeral?"

Jack G. said, "I couldn't tell you that for pure love nor hard money. Leeper's a crazy coot to start with, and he just lost his kid. So I don't know if he's okay or not."

We were through town and up on the big curve by the sawmill already. I'd never had a faster trip through Union.

I kept pushing. "Did you . . . uh, did you hear anybody talking about the funeral? About what I said at the funeral?"

Jack G. looked over at me. "What? Oh, yeah, people are talkin' about it, all right."

"I mean, what are they saying? Is anybody . . . uh, are there some people not believing what I said?"

"Not believin'?" He looked at me. "I heard one or two."

I waited. "Who was it? What did they say?"

"It was just a couple people. But they was shootin' off their mouths, goin' on. I told 'em they'd be wise to keep their ideas on this subject to theirselves." The deputy slowed and made the turn off the highway onto the dirt road up Roan Creek.

Maybe Jerry was right. Maybe nobody believed me. Maybe I was the biggest possible fool for what I'd done and had only made things worse. And what had I done to Jerry? He'd tried to tell me, and I didn't want to hear it. I'd hurt him, as if that would keep people believing.

We were almost home, moving fast down the hill past my great-uncle Vic's house, when Jack G. said quietly, "That's a helluva thing you did there today, son. Took some guts, I'll say that. Thing of it is, you don't really have to worry who believed you. There's only one man on God's green earth needs to believe you. Only one."

At the house, the Dodge was out front and Dad was sitting on the porch. He'd already changed clothes, and the sprinkler was running. Keno stood up from the shade and barked when we pulled in, until he saw it was me and lay back down.

Dad was glad to see me, I could tell. Jack G. came up to the porch with me. He and Dad talked.

"Dale, I'm goin' to stay awhile," Jack G. said. I was glad to hear it. "But I think I'll ditch the truck. No use havin' it out in plain sight. That way, when Leeper comes by and doesn't know I'm here, we'll see if he has somethin' in mind."

Dad opened one gate and I opened the other,

and Jack G. drove his truck out of sight behind the woodshed.

We were all back on the porch when Keno perked up his ears and looked down the river road. In a few seconds, we heard it, too. It was Arlie's truck coming around the bend. Jack G. stood up and went inside where he wouldn't be seen. He called Dad and me to come in, too.

We watched from the living room window, staying out of sight. Keno ran to the yard gate to bark a couple of times. Arlie looked our way and slowed down—either to make the sharp turn up the Branagan road or to turn in and accuse us. Then he made the turn and headed on home.

It must have worked! I breathed again. It was like the world was lifted off my shoulders.

"Well," Jack G. said. "Looks good, I guess."

"That's a relief," Dad said.

Jack G. looked at me. "Looks like your words mighta worked, boy."

We went back to the porch and sat down on the davenport.

"I'll wait awhile and see that Leeper don't come back," Jack G. said.

Jack G. started on a story about a car wreck he'd tended to a few days ago. A man from out of town had a few too many to drink, lost control, and drove his car into a shallow part of the river on the Emmett road. He was sitting on top of it, high and dry, playing a harmonica and drinking another beer, when Jack G. came by to rescue him. When that story was done, I went out and moved the sprinkler.

I came back, and while I wanted to listen to more of Jack G.'s stories, I decided to do the afternoon chores while he was still here. It would help Dad, and it seemed better to do them now in case Arlie did come back.

I went in to change clothes and from inside I heard Jack G. say something about a headstone. I finished tying my shoes and went toward the porch to hear what they were talking about. Before I got there, I heard Jack G. say, "Craziest thing I ever saw—people forkin' over money for a thing like that."

I didn't know what he was talking about, and I reached for the screen door to go out and hear more. But then he started up again talking about the harmonica man he helped out of the river. I could ask Dad about the headstone later. So I went out back and started on chores.

I started with the chickens and threw the grain out on the ground. They came running and flapping and squawking—selfish beggars, like most animals are when they eat with their friends. I watched them awhile, studying their quick head movements and noisy eating.

Across the creek at the barn, the cow met me and I settled into the rhythm of milking. My hands would hurt before I was through if I didn't pace myself. I was barely started when I heard a vehicle. I stood up and looked out the barn door. It was Jack G.'s truck pulling through the first gate. Dad was opening the second one for him. I didn't like it. I wanted him to stay longer.

I went back to milking and tried to hurry. But it felt slow. At last, I finished and let the cow out. When I started for the house, Dad was going in the back door with the egg basket.

I'd made it to the middle of our little bridge when I was stopped cold by Keno letting out a sudden and tremendous yammering from the yard. I looked up and saw a figure at our front gate. There was no vehicle of any kind, but I saw instantly who it was.

The bucket left my hand and hit the edge of the bridge like a lead weight, shooting a long geyser of milk out over the creek in slow motion. Before the milk even hit the water I was gone, running like a madman for the house.

I was out of breath when I hit the back door, looking for Dad. Just then, I heard the front screen slam. Through it, I saw Dad leaving the porch and crossing the yard to meet Arlie Leeper. He told Keno to quiet down. Arlie opened the gate and came into the yard.

It looked like we were wrong about Arlie's change for the better. He wouldn't stop by just for a social call. In all the times he came collecting for the water, he'd never set foot inside our door. Even in the coldest weather, he'd stand on the porch while Mom got the check ready, in spite of her importunings to come in. Social, he wasn't.

And now, he'd watched and waited until the deputy left, then he'd snuck up on us, keeping quiet by parking his truck somewhere up the creek and walking the rest of the way.

Arlie was almost to where Dad stood. I wanted to go out, but I was breathing hard from running, and I stood there trying to catch my breath. And then, I had another idea. I pushed the open door nearly closed, and there was Mom's .30-30 still leaning in the corner from last night. I picked it up. It felt good in my hands.

I almost wanted Arlie to see the rifle, but I decided against it and stood behind the door where I could still see and hear through the crack. I didn't know what I was going to do, but I knew one thing for sure: Arlie Leeper wouldn't be hurting my dad today.

Arlie was saying something about taking his kids home and stopping his truck up the road. I strained to hear. "Took and walked on down 'cause I didn't know the deputy was here or not." He fidgeted with his hands. "Now, what I come to say—well, I didn't believe your boy today. He told the truth about the fire in my fence a few days back. He told the truth then, all right, but today, at the funeral, when he said that about my boy Dennis savin' him and all, that didn't sound like somethin' to be believed at first. That just didn't seem real. Thought it must be a trick."

I clutched the rifle in both hands. I envisioned myself jumping through the door and pointing it at Arlie and telling him to get away from us. One threatening word and I'd do it.

He went on. "Thought it was a trick 'cause I

couldn't see my boy a hero. Couldn't. But then, you know, the preacher told me over at the graveyard that people in the town, they took and they started up a collection. They was raisin' money and it was for a cemetery stone for my boy. I was real surprised at that. Just couldn't imagine a thing like that." Dad nodded, and while I didn't understand, I remembered what the deputy had said about collecting money.

I missed a few words and leaned closer to hear Arlie say in his slow, rambling way, ". . . sort of a monument. The preacher, he called it a monument, for the town hero my boy turned out to be, you know. And they want to put on it what he done and all. Take and write on it what he done to save your boy." His voice cracked, and he drew his fingertips across his eyes in a quick motion.

A meteorite could have blasted into the yard with an inscribed message from martians on it right then and I couldn't have been any more stupefied. A monument for Dennis Leeper? How could it be?

"I heard about it, Arlie," Dad said. "From the deputy."

I noticed that Arlie was talking more softly today, and his face didn't have his usual scowl. "And, well, sometimes, maybe I ain't very quick. But when that happened, why, then I knew. People wouldn't do all that if my boy wasn't a hero, now would they? When that happened, then I knew your boy tol' the truth. They wouldn't give out money if it wasn't true. And people wouldn't take and clap their hands at a funeral like that for somebody that wasn't a real hero, now would they? So then, I knew it was true. It just had to be true, what your boy said."

Dad stared at him. I couldn't believe what I was hearing. And I knew I had to be with Dad. I set the rifle behind the door and went outside to stand beside him.

Arlie looked at me and said, "I just was tellin' your dad that, at first, I didn't believe what you said today. I couldn't. But then, when people told me about collectin' money for the monument, then I knew it was true."

His eyes were settled down more than I'd ever seen them, looking right at us. And I couldn't get over how different he looked, shaved and cleaned up, still in his funeral clothes.

He said, "A monument. Can you imagine?" He paused to think about it. "First, when my boy died, well, I just wanted to get even. With you. The town. Everybody. That's what I wanted most in the world. But that wasn't right. No, no. Now I know that wasn't right." He shook his head several times.

"So all that I said the other night 'bout gettin' even and all, why, that was just talk. Foolish talk. You can forget about all that. I wouldn't never do them things. None of 'em."

Sometimes, there are no words, and Dad and I had none now.

Arlie looked at me. "I thank you for what you did today."

I made myself look right at him. I said, "Yes, sir. You're welcome."

Arlie was done. His lips curled up in a tiny, sad smile, the very first I'd ever seen from him. He turned slightly, like he was ready to go. "You both take and put this behind you now. It's over. You're a good man, Dale, your family and all. It's over for good. I don't know what more to say. It's just plain all over now, the end of the line. You put it away."

Dad mumbled some words of thanks and blessing and reached out to shake Arlie's hand. Arlie accepted the gesture, but looked clumsy at it. He shook mine, too. Then he turned and quickly walked away. We watched him walk out the gate and start up his road.

seventeen

Dad turned to me. His hug was quick and hard and rare. It felt good. I looked at his face. He started to say something, but could only shake his head. Good as we both felt, no words were needed.

In a moment, the ringing phone sliced through the mood. Dad went inside and answered it. I followed him as far as the porch. I could tell he was talking to Mom, telling her what had happened.

I listened to most of it, trying to keep the good feeling, but when the talk wore on, I got to thinking about all that had happened today.

I went to find the milk bucket. It was lying in the shallow creek bottom, dented in two places from where it hit the rocks in the creek, but no worse for wear. Milk was spattered on the rocks for twenty feet downstream. I brought in the bucket and washed it out at the kitchen sink. Dad was still on the phone, telling the story again, so I figured he must now be talking to somebody else. I listened from the kitchen as I worked, and I could tell it was Aunt Lois; Dad had a special, lilting way of talking to his sister that made me know.

I decided to feed the pigs, so I went to the granary and got pig feed in a bucket and went out across the road. Keno tagged along. I leaned on the fence for a time, watching the hogs eat and thinking. It wasn't so hot now and the clouds were nearly gone.

I heard a vehicle coming from town. I didn't want to see anybody right now, so I called to Keno to follow. We quickly crossed the bridge and turned up the curve of the road to the Leepers', where it started its climb alongside the creek and where we'd be out of sight of the main road.

Through the trees, I saw the pastor's older Buick turn in to our place. I wondered what he was doing here until I saw Mom and Marie get out. The three of them went into the house.

I knew I should go back home, and it didn't seem right to hide from the pastor, but still I didn't want to face anyone right now. I had some figuring to do first.

Keno and I stopped at the wide place in the road, the same spot where Dad and I had come less than a week before to check on the Leepers' fence. It was here that I'd skipped rocks in the dust, and it was here that we'd had our confrontation with Arlie. That day seemed like it belonged to another world. Since then, everything had changed, and I didn't feel like rock throwing anymore.

I sat down on the edge of the road above the creek and scratched Keno's ears while I waited for the pastor to leave. The dog had been neglected the last few days and needed a little attention. He lay his head across my lap and closed his eyes.

The evening shadows of the trees were now skinny, groping fingers covering the road in a tangle as thick as my thoughts.

Now that things had turned out good with Arlie, I should be happy. I'd got what I wanted. But it was all starting to feel bittersweet, like when you catch a beautiful and shining trout and you're excited, but at the same time you're sad, because it had to die and its beauty fades by the minute. I was glad about Arlie, but my heart was hurting.

I had to wonder what kind of boy I'd become. One thing I knew, and I didn't like it: I was now a boy who could stand up and tell a lie right in front of everyone, right in front of the pastor, right in front of God.

I'd stood up to tell people that Arlie was after us, and while I stood there and saw the truth not working, I changed the whole thing and told a complete and enormous lie.

I knew lying was wrong and I'd always hated it. I couldn't make myself feel good about it ever, not even today.

But I knew this: I'd do it again if I had to.

That was the most amazing thing—to know I could do it again, no matter how it made me feel or what people thought.

A boy who would deliberately lie was a different boy than I had been. I didn't like that. But I would live with it, because that's how things now were. There was no way back.

The sun had dropped quite a ways and the light was turning yellow before Keno's ears popped up. I stood up and saw the pastor's car pull away and head back toward town.

"Come on, boy," I called to Keno, and we headed down the road. I picked up the bucket at the pigpen, rinsed it at the hose, and put it on the back porch. I didn't go in the house. I had one more thing to do.

The sun was down now—going down a little earlier each night—and there was a touch of coolness in the air that hadn't been there other evenings. It reminded me that fall was almost here and school less than two weeks away.

In the granary, I found the old hunting knife we kept there. I went around behind the woodshed and into the brush below the logjam. Keno didn't follow this time but went early to his night spot on the back porch. A lone cricket by the clothesline started his evening song.

I sat a long time on the old, whitened log and looked out across the quiet water, my fingers moving on Jerry's inscription.

RAFT   AUG 57
JERRY JAMIE

I sat and thought about everything as best I could. Finally, it felt right. I'd make my own monument.

Kneeling, I took the knife and right beside my own name, carefully carved in:

DENNIS

I was hurrying to use the light I had and the handle of the knife wore my palm sore. I tried to match Jerry's letters and make the new word look like it fit in, like it had been there all along. I wanted it to be right.

I was almost finished when I heard footsteps behind me.

"I saw you come down this way," Dad said. "Mom and Marie are here. The pastor brought them." He came over and knelt beside me, leaning in close to read the carving in the dim light. He looked surprised, then nodded slowly when he saw what I was doing. He studied my face.

"How are you doing, Jamie? We didn't get to talk after Arlie left. We didn't get to talk hardly at all today."

"Okay, I guess," I said with a sigh.

"You did a lot of good today," he said, after a pause. "You brought out the good in Arlie. It could be a turning point for him. I think it might be."

I turned and absently went back to perfecting my carving. A little time passed. "I guess you know," I said abruptly. "I guess you know I lied." I hadn't even planned to say it.

After a moment, he said softly, "I guess I do."

"I guess near everybody knows," I said. I stopped working with the knife and looked at him. "Never once after we went over the dam did I touch Dennis or see him or even know where he was in that terrible, wild water. I lost my can and grabbed another one—that's true—but it was just a loose one. Dennis had nothing to do with it."

My voice was shaky, but it kept coming out.

"I lied. I didn't know what else to do. It was the hardest thing I ever did. But it seemed like it didn't matter right then if it was right or wrong. With Arlie's threats and all . . ."

My voice was getting high and full of tears, and I tried to calm myself down. I turned away and went back to the carving for a moment to hide my face.

Dad watched me work, then said, "Some things in life are hard to sort out." He rubbed his cheek. "But it's done now. And this is important—you didn't lie to save yourself, like ninety-nine percent of the lies in the world. You did it to save me—and all of us—from Arlie's wrath. I know that. You did what you thought was right in a tough situation. That's all any man can ask of another."

When I had my voice more under control, I said, "The people in town, it hurt me bad inside to lie to them."

"They understand, Jamie," he said.

"They didn't believe me, did they?" I asked. "Jerry tried to tell me. But I couldn't stand that—to hear him say they didn't believe me. So I wasn't fair to him."

Dad said, "Well, I don't know that story, but the pastor told me that Jerry said tonight he's ready to slug any kid who doubts you. You know how Jerry talks."

I wanted to smile and cry at the same time, hearing that—knowing that Jerry would stick by me after the mean thing I'd done to him.

Dad moved to sit on the log. "You heard about the headstone, the money collected?" he said.

"Why would people do that, Dad, when they didn't believe me?"

"They're willing to share this with you," Dad said. "They heard about Arlie's threats, and this was their way of helping."

I could hardly see Dad's face in the darkness, except the light in his eyes.

I laid the knife on the log. "I didn't know . . . I just didn't know people would be like that." I shook my head and said, "Life is so funny."

Nobody spoke for a time. Then Dad said, "Go ahead and finish, Jamie. You've got a good start."

I picked up the knife and went back to work. It took only a few minutes. "There," I said.

It was too dark to see by the time I finished, but Dad reached over and felt the letters I'd made. I didn't know how they felt to his fingers, but they felt good to my heart.

Dad said, "Life *is* funny, Jamie. But I know one thing—life has a way of seeing what we're made of. It pulls us into things, pulls tricks on us, gives us impossible choices, changes the rules, does everything in the world to make things hard, then watches to see what we'll do."

Dad paused and I nodded, thinking about his words.

Suddenly, he gave a single little sound like the start of a laugh. "Life kicked you today," he said, "but you kicked back real good!"

We sat silent, listening to the murmur of the dark and unchanging river. I felt better now. There was more to say, it felt like, but I didn't know how to say it. Dad had run out of words, too. It seemed like that was how life was getting to be lately—complicated and having things inside that didn't know how to get out.

Finally, Dad stood up and said, "Are you ready to come in now? Your mom will want to see you."

Dad put his hand on my shoulder as we started to the house. He waited for me while I stopped at the granary to put away the knife.

On the way back to the house, we stopped to look at the night. It was a fine one. Several stars were already out in a clear sky. It was good to see them, bright and sharp and in their right places. And crickets all over were singing now.

Up past the house and the walnut trees, I could barely make out the black fire scar on the hill. I wondered how long it would take for new growth to cover the burn. Even now, after the storm of the other night, a few blades of grass might be daring to start up. I'd check tomorrow morning.

The kitchen light cast a warm patch of gold through the window onto the backyard grass. The curtains were open, and I could see Mom moving back and forth between the refrigerator and the table. She'd be setting out bread, milk, fruit, and cheese—our usual simple supper after such a long day. She wiped her hands on her apron and came to the door and opened it, looking for us and waiting.

Marie was standing on a chair at the stove, rhythmically shaking a pan with a lid back and forth, and through the open window I could hear the tiny, muffled explosions of popping corn. It surprised me that the sound alone could make me hungry, but it did. Oh, it did.

Keno stood up from his bed and looked at us from the porch, to see if he was missing something, like he couldn't imagine what was keeping us.

We headed for the open door.